CW01497160

It's About a Murder,

Cariad

Byron Kalies

ISBN: 1514144999
ISBN-13: 978-1514144992

CONTENTS

Friday July 14th 1933

CONTENTS

Saturday July 8th 1933

CONTENTS

Sunday July 9th 1933

ACKNOWLEDGMENTS

Cover photograph – Alys Kalies

THE VICTOR'S TALE

'Then war broke out in heaven. Michael and his angels fought against the dragon, and the dragon and his angels fought back. But he was not strong enough, and they lost their place in heaven. The great dragon was hurled down--that ancient serpent called the devil, or Satan, who leads the whole world astray. He was hurled to the earth, and his angels with him.' - ***Revelation 12:7 -9***

THE LEADER'S TALE

I was hurt, physically and mentally. Amos managed the physical but the mental scars took a longer time to repair. But they healed and I'm healthy now, stronger, fitter, wiser. I'm more careful, more prepared. But let me tell you my side of the story.

First, some background -

He creates beautiful women on earth, so beautiful that angels are attracted to them and marry them and have children. Then He decides that He made a mistake and orders the angels to turn on each other. 'Then war broke out in heaven.' Yes it did. The war between compliance and love. The war between His robots and the passionate ones who, let's not forget, He created to exercise their own free will. A war between fire and dishwater. A war between the angels that couldn't pull and the angels that could. It should have been a no-brainer really. But, we lost and the meek did inherit the fucking earth after all.

My question. What type of God is it that allows these things to happen? I'll tell you what God shall I? On a judging these behaviours sliding scale, where the bottom end of the scale is - uh inconsistent. I would put the top of the scale at somewhere between spiteful and downright evil. That's right. I said it. OK. It may be just sour grapes because we lost, but really.

And why did we lose? We lost due to the actions of one. One powerful one. Ironically a friend, a good friend. He was a begater. He begat my wife's sister. And they were very happy until He butted in and decided it was all a mistake. A sin. Then my begating friend decided to swap sides. He switched from the passion to the dull. And did He notice? He who is all-seeing, all powerful. Did he see? Well, apparently not. The fact that my friend the bagater could call on a thousand or so troops was

4

irrelevant was it?

I am bitter. True. But I am also a leader and lead the defeated away and to here - Mynydd Eimon, Wales. Some asked me why? Why Mynydd Eimon, Wales? I answer - why not? If it were Turkey or Syria would it be better?

How long ago was it? Time is a difficult concept for us. It's more a circle than a straight line. We get on, we get off. We cut across, go back, go forward. Time is overrated.

'All truth is crooked, time itself is a circle.'

FRIDAY JULY 14th 1933

1 Funeral

The heavens had opened. It was a black day. Cold. Wet. Thundery. Black. Harsh. Welsh November rain. Clichéd dark black sky.

It was the funeral of Cai Tywysog, twenty three year old golf professional of Mynydd Eimon Golf Club. He had been accidentally shot by Aunty Mary in a freak, premeditated accident involving an army revolver. She had admitted this and everyone believed her. Aunty Mary would never lie.

'Nice crowd', my uncle Daniel muttered to me as we stood cold and sodden at the graveside. I looked at him in bewilderment. 'No!' it wasn't a nice crowd in any sense. There were barely a dozen people present even if you included my dead best friend, the gravediggers and the priest. I checked my watch again. We had been here twenty minutes already waiting for the priest to show up. He had disappeared somewhere between the church and the graveyard.

I looked around, again. It wasn't a particularly nice, or happy, crowd. We were lined up along the side of the grave in the cold, wet rain with not one umbrella between us. For some reason no-one like kids at a school dance - males to the right, females to the left. On the right hand side the four male mourners were staring at the ground looking like a bad marketing idea of reuniting the original film cast of Reservoir Dogs forty years later. Our black suits were, well, disparate. Mine was new and fitted the occasion with style and a certain elegance, if I say so myself. The others looked like they had been dragged out from the back of three ancient wardrobes the previous evening and shoved under the mattress to press last night. The new identical black ties were just... well too new. They were as obvious as something new on an old thing.

The men were arranged in weight order in front of me. First and weighing in at around 10 stone was the headmaster, Dr Pedwar Penn. Pedwar remarked, quite cheerfully, 'Mae hi'n bwrw hen wragedd a ffyn.' I looked sharply at him as I had a decent understand of the Welsh language but had never been that wonderful at it in school, ironically taught by him. 'It's raining old ladies and sticks, so it is.' I forced a painful pretend smile then looked around. The other sodden faces hadn't even made that much effort. Next to Pedwar, stood the doctor - Dr Amos Caddoc. Then came Uncle Daniel and finally yours truly. Not that I was the heaviest. I meant the men's weight leading up to me. I would probably fit somewhere between Pedwar and Amos. I like things to be correct.

I looked up at the bizarre reflective image standing across from us, across the coffin. It was like two teams waiting in a tunnel to run out at Cardiff Arms Park to do mortalish rugby combat. Or, if I looked more kindly it seemed nothing more than the school hall at the first school dance. However, on reflection, I felt the best version would be that if we were on the dexter side of the coffin, the sinister side looked, well, even more 'from the pen of Charles Addams'. This femina side contained, from the head of the deceased to his shoes; my sister, Seren; my receptionist, Lily, although she preferred the title secretary; Dr Amos' receptionist, Rose; and the murderer herself, Auntie Mary.

It seemed that from the head end to the toe end of the crate the women had been arranged in age and height order. My sister, Seren was the tallest, and youngest. She looked like the young actress Carolyn Jones in her early days, playing the original Morticia Adams. Next came Lily, who managed to look under dressed and overdressed at the same time in a short black number. Rose looked exactly what she was - an aggressive doctor's receptionist. Although I gathered, she preferred to be known as a secretary also. Which left the smallest and oldest - Aunty Mary. Aunty Mary was as old as the grave, which was appropriate at this time and withered like an old apple-john. She had always looked this old though. I had known her ever since I was a baby, and she looked ready to pop her clogs then.

Lily was the odd one out of these four sirens, or harpies depending on your perspective. She showed flashes of real emotion. She was sad and sniffing and actually holding back a few tears. This struck me as unusual. In the ten days she had been my unpaid, unasked for receptionist she had been solid and dependable and as emotion-free as the other mourners. Rose held her hand tightly and whispered 'shh' a good many times. Seren looked totally pissed off and glared at the sky and the rain. She also glared at the coffin and at Lily every time she breathed. Aunty Mary, well she was just Aunty Mary. She was emotionless, unfathomable, soaking wet and as empty as Satan's heart.

Two other shapes dressed in Reservoir Dogs attire appeared pathetically holding their collars against the rain. These were two characters I had been forced to attend Balaclava Road School (mixed) with for just over a decade. They were brothers. They were twins. They were twin brothers. They were Dai Proper, the eldest and Dai Copy, the next eldest. I went to Balaclava Road School (mixed) with them for the best part of sixteen years. They looked nothing like each other. They were of similar disposition though - both filled with that traditional Welsh miserablist outlook on life. The outlook where poets write of, 'Dead man naked being one with the man in the wind and the west moon'. They were both, as my sister, Seren described them, in less poetic terms, 'as thicker than pig shit and twice as loathsome.' They worked for my Uncle, Daniel, and 'helped out'. I dreaded to think what that entailed. But, they seemed to like it. Well, as much as they appeared to enjoy anything in their strange, curious entwined, little lives. They moved together toward the coffin in that oddly affected Liam Gallagher walk they have been practising since they were twelve. Then they separated and locomoted to

9

either side of the coffin. Dai Copy plonked himself between Amos and Uncle Daniel whilst Dai Proper shrugged and elbow a gap between the set of secretaries. They took up the ropes that lay under the coffin and gently, gently, breathtakingly gently they astonishingly, almost scarily, lowered the box skilfully into the hole. The only sound, apart from Lily's intermittent sobbing, and the quietest of squeaks from the ropes, was the fitful grumbling and cursing of Dai Proper as he worked. With the tiniest bump it was over, the eagle had landed, and they moved away.

We all exhaled as one. I looked up and Father Barry had appeared and was speaking. Father Barry was tall and skinny. He looked like a very tall, angry praying mantis with rain dripping off his nose. He was dressed all in off-white priest garb and had the three day stubble of a tramp, or a reunion tour rock star. He mumbled and looked down, always down. I was mesmerised - not in a good way. He was another Mynydd Eimon person who looked any age between seventy and three hundred and seventy. I was close enough to smell him. He smelt of whiskey, incense and the bible.

He slurred and stuttered and spoke, not loudly nor quietly. He spoke in an apologetic conversational voice that people could hear, but needed to strain themselves to separate one word from the next. If anyone not from the village were listened, which would never, ever happen, they would just hear a drone, a hum of soporific white noise.

The first sentence I picked out was, 'Man is full of misery.' With that bombshell he stopped. He looked down at a battered, bach, black indeterminate book. He paused. He looked up expeditiously then back down. He continued, 'He cometh up and is cut down like a flower.' He paused again. He put his hand into his pocket and blindly sprinkled dirt onto the coffin. 'In the midst of life they are in death.' Another pause. 'Deliver them not into the bitter pains of eternal death.' A longer pause as he looked at his book for inspiration. 'Oh man, thou wert dust and hast returned to dust today.' He stopped. He looked exhausted.

I recognised that I was irritated and getting more and more and more annoyed. I was wet, not that much of a surprise for someone born in a South Wales valley village, and annoyed, irritated and pissed off. I was annoyed at the fact that I had had to wear a new suit and shiny black tie. I was irritated that Father Barry had taken a long, long time to turn up for the ceremony - thirty three minutes. I was pissed off with my best friend Cai for dying. Still, I couldn't blame him really. He was dead. And well it wasn't entirely his fault. He didn't ask to be shot.

Father Barry continued, 'Happy from now on.' Another pause. 'Sweat of thy shiny face. Bread.' He stopped. He looked at the eight miserable, wet faces around the coffin and shrugged apologetically to us. He charged on, 'We commit the body of Cai Twswygog to the ground.' He stopped one more time, took a deep breath and charged at the finishing line, 'earth to earth, dust to dust, eternal to life. Mercy. Bless him. Amen.'

There was a general mumbling, grumbling, rumbling chorus of 'Amens' from the mourners. Then a rather too loud 'A fucking men.' from Seren.

I needed a cigarette.

2 Flashback Friday July 7th 1933

I opened the door of my Balaclava Road office at my usual time, nine o'clock precisely. I liked things to be right. I like things to be where they should be. I didn't have a long commute to the office so had no excuse to be late, not that I had a boss to answer to anyway. I lived above my office and had followed my usual routine. I had left my house ten minutes ago, walked along Alma Road and Malakoff Street where I had picked up two packets of Lucky Strikes at Mrs Evans' corner shop. I had nodded to Cai Twswygog who was going into the shop as I left, then returned on the same route to my office. I smiled at the exquisite lettering on the door of the office, 'Samael K. Watcher ... Investigations'. I didn't have a middle name but thought the 'K' added a touch of class. I passed through the waiting room where Lily, my receptionist sat between nine thirty and five, less the hour I gave her for lunch, which she had never taken. 'Waiting room' was perhaps too grand a phrase for what was essentially a tiny front room in a mining terraced house hidden deep in a Welsh valley. More a holding pen. The pen had a desk with a phone. It was functional. The desk was old, solid and grey. Uncle Daniel had found it somewhere and someone had delivered it. It was exactly to my specification. I wasn't particularly creative when it came to interior design but I knew what I like. Even a minimalist interior design would have added a few more features to the room.

I opened the door of my inner office. I stepped inside. As I say I like things to be just so and they weren't. The room contained a second hand desk, two old, old, grey chairs (one moved, one in the process of being sat on), a wall safe, a fireplace without a fire, a bit of light grey carpet, a coat stand with coat and bonnet, and a visitor. Everything was neat, tidy and functional. I looked around slowly, carefully. I breathed. I walked across the room in a business-like manner and placed myself in my violated chair behind my desk and looked at my visitor.

She was a frail old woman dressed in a long black dress, grey shawl, and tight bun with a lethal looking hair slide. From the back she seemed very peaceful as she stared down into the empty fireplace, in some kind of geriatric trance. She seemed to have made herself completely at home. I reached in my pocket to get a cigarette, looked at the woman and thought better of it. I picked up a pen from my desk and started twirling it in my fingers. I had been having problems remembering things but I had no difficulty remembering this dame. I breathed, 'Aunty Mary', I said a little too loudly, 'What are you doing here?'

She moved her head toward me as she started speaking, as if she really did have eyes in the back of her head. 'It's about a murder, cariad. I'm ashamed to say. It's about the murder of young Cai.' She stared straight at me.

'Cai!' I feigned astonishment for some reason, then continued, 'but I've seen him just now in Mrs Evans'.'

She thought for a minute, then corrected herself, 'well the murder may not be Cai and anyway it's not today.'

'I see.' I clearly didn't. I sucked hard on my pen in a way that I thought may convey serious thoughtfulness.

'So what is it you want from me?' I enquired as professionally as I could.

'I need some information, some advice if you will.'

'Shoot'.

'How am I looking if I were to murder someone?' she asked thoughtfully.

I sat down and continued working on my thoughtful expression,

13

'I imagine you should be put in jail Aunty Mary.'

'Ah,' she paused, 'we both know that's not going to happen.' She re framed the question for me, 'I'm more concerned for my soul, cariad?'

'Well,' I paused. 'That would be one for you and the priest to negotiate.'

She looked disappointed, 'and the soul of the victim?'

'Again your priest would be the one to talk to there.'

'Not you?' she asked hopefully, I felt.

I had to disappoint her, 'Not me.'

'Are you sure about that?'

'Pretty sure.'

'Any road,' she continued, 'I'd like you to investigate the murder, when it happens. Would you do that for me, Samael?'

I nodded professionally.

'Thank you Samael,' she continued talking as she eased herself up, fairly painfully, I felt, 'You've been very helpful. Now how much do I owe you?'

'Aunty Mary you know I couldn't take money off you.'

'You're a sweet boy.' she said as she reached up and ruffled my hair. She handed me a shilling piece, 'Now take it and let's hear no more about it.'

I took my retainer and helped Aunty Mary put on her ancient grey fur coat and black bonnet.

Something about the musky, old womanly smell of it, reminded me of the many occasions I had helped her on with this when I was growing up. This coat used to scare me. She did however frequently have sweets in the left hand pocket and I could feel my hand inadvertently reaching into the pocket. I stopped myself. I shivered slightly then I walked Aunty Mary out.

14

3 Wake

The clocks had been stopped in the only pub in the village, 'The Lamb'.
The mirrors were turned to the wall. There were six old, wooden tables
spread out around the pub. Each table had six or seven tables
surrounding it. It was traditional. The pub could have been the venue for
a wake for eight hundred years or more. Nothing has changed. It was
the way it had always been. The walls are still stone and cold. The
beams are low and exposed. The corners are dark and secretive. The bar
staff are apathetic and grumpy. The customers are as mercenary as
ever. There were a lot more people in the pub than were at the church.
This is the traditional Welsh custom of never knowingly missing a free
meal or drink. Even with thirty or forty people present it was quiet.
People were wearing black, smoking, drinking and eating sandwiches.
Most were attempting to look respectfully sad. It was still early though.
The Ray Noble Orchestra's *The Very Thought of You* played in the
background.

 I'm Sam, by the way. Samael Watcher. Mid-twenties... ish, or so
I believe. Son of Sam - senior. Son of Ishtar - disappeared. Brother of
Seren - foul mouthed sister. Scratch golfer. Private investigator. Former
Grand Slam winning golfer Bobby Jones. But more of that later.

 I lifted my glass of Four Roses whiskey from the bar, dragged on
my Lucky Strike and looked around the crowded, smoky pub. On the far
side of the lounge (lounge? - It was the big room in the pub. It was the
bar in the day and the lounge in the evening) I could see my sister. She
looked like her old, lugubrious self. She was leaning against a wall in her
elegant black dress drinking gin and smoking. She was talking, or rather,
she was, listening to Lily. This wasn't a competence my sister was
particularly gifted at. I didn't need to even see, or hear Seren to know

what mood she was in, on two counts. Firstly she was something of an open book - WYSIWYG. Also, a good ninety five percent of the time she was angry. She listened to Lily and I could see her very limited level of patience draining as rapidly as confidence after a poorly struck putt. Lily seemed oblivious and concentrated on being upset. She was animated, talking very loudly, yet still managing to drink consistently. She was smoking as well, something I never knew she did. She slurred and spouted and smoked with vast hand gestures and was jabbing her finger at Seren. Detective that I am, I sensed there would be trouble before long. My sister looked carefully at Lily, said something cuspidate then turned her head away and looked at our Uncle Daniel.

Uncle Daniel was sitting near the door holding court like Charles Laughton in Henry VIII or a squashed, obese Don Corleone. He caught Seren's look, stood up very quickly and walked across the room to Lily. He grabbed hold of her hands and calmed her down with soothing words, I assume. I couldn't hear him over the din of the music and the grazing of the crowd. Uncle Daniel gently eased her towards the furthest table where Aunty Mary and Pedwar Penn sit like bookends. He pulled up a seat and plonked Lily down on it, instructing her to, 'sit and behave'. I could lip-read that part. He hovered over her to check if she would. She did. Obviously satisfied with his domination and influencing skills he moved back to his regal table and awaiting retinue. This was an elegant performance from my uncle. He is not the most nimble of people, resembling, as he does, Kasper Gutman from the film of the Maltese Falcon. I was surprised and impressed to see him in action. I realised now that my descriptions are practically all cinematically related. I watch a lot of films. It's one of the (few) delights and perks of being the son of an angel. Time, being curved, or circular may occasionally have vortexes and become nebulous. Not frequently, or dramatically, and never enough to 'leave external aspects inconsistent or enlightened in any significant way'. Or so I was taught by Mr. Penn at Balaclava Road School (mixed).

I blinked, shook these thoughts off and returned to Uncle Daniel. My Uncle Daniel. Daniel Llewellyn. Solicitor. I had barely spoke to him since my return to the village. The only time I had had a decent conversation was on my first evening. I was sitting in the elegant living room of his elegant house. I had no idea how I had got there, or how long I had been there. I remember my mouth opening and closing and realised that I was talking. It was incredibly unsettling. Usually I am pretty articulate. I am an educated young man who went to school, did well and later spent seven years in Augusta, America. I can talk. Fluently. Most of the time. It was a little like being drunk, but not. When you're drunk you sort of know it and compensate, or over compensate. This was just like being above yourself watching some idiot try to speak. I remember telling Uncle Daniel that I wanted to be a private eye and would like an office, a receptionist, a hat and a gun. I described each requirement from the film 'The Maltese Falcon'. Uncle Daniel said, 'I'll see what I can do,' and lo and behold it all just happened.

Since returning from America a few weeks ago, I have been prone to lapses of memory, or more accurately prone to periods of remembering. It is getting better quite quickly. I have few problems now remembering the past week or so. I have superb recollection of my first sixteen years growing up in Mynydd Eimon. It's the years in Augusta and the how I got there and how I returned that seem to trouble me. There's also about three years since I left Augusta that I have no idea about. I'm not overly worried by all of this. Which in itself should be a little worrying. It's a little frustrating and occasionally painful when I remember some details about a wife and three children I had a few years ago. I do have headaches and bad dreams almost constantly. Uncle Daniel told me they would go away. Uncle Daniel is full of shit.

I was bored looking at Uncle Daniel so swung my head around in

17

a slow pan of the room until I found my sister again. She was looking bored now. She still leaned against the wall, smoking and listless. I stare at her. I managed to catch her eye and flick my head nonchalantly toward the door. She coolly dropped her cigarette, crunched it under her elegant black shoe and walked toward the side door I am flicking toward.

4 Brother and Sister

In the gwli between the pub and 14 Taganrog Terrace, Seren and I conversed properly for the first time in many years (around ten would seem a reasonable estimate). It had stopped raining but the path with still wet and glistening. Not in a glistening, shimmering way. More in a wet, dull, grim, grey, cigarette-strewn way. My sister was leaning up against the pub wall. She took a Lucky Strike from me, lit it with a small silver lighter and inhaled deeply. She looked as fed up as I was. She looked around at the place we were in. It was pretty bleak. She looked like she was about to cry. She was a year older than me and at least ten years smarter. I didn't think she was going to cry at the joy of talking to me again though. It was something else. From past experience I understood that as direct as Seren was, she didn't response too well to direct questions herself.

She was my chwaer, my older sister, my protector. I had a reputation, in my early years, for being a bit of a mummy's boy. She had a reputation for being a little, well, more than a little.... forthright. She had stayed in the village for every minute of her all her life, baring the very occasional shopping trip to Cardiff or holiday in Porthcawl. I, on the other hand had somehow become a famous international jet-setter for seven years or so whilst inhabited the body of Grand Slam winning golfer Bobby Jones. Our relationship would inevitably be changed. I wondered if I were still her baby brother, her Sammy Bach.

We smoked our cigarettes both lost in our own little worlds, separately but right next to each other waiting for the other to make the first move. Dai Proper, a twin, walked past me. He stopped and turned to me.

'Sam', he shook my hand warmly, 'How are you butt?'

'Not bad, Dai. Not bad.'

'Seren. How are things Seren?' His gaze moved to Seren's chest. Not for long, but just long enough.

'Oy Dai!' she pointed to her face, 'I'm up here.'

'Sorry cariad.'

'Don't you fucking cariad me Dai Proper, you little shit.'

Dai Proper promptly shuffled back to the sanctuary of 'The Lamb'.

'Twll tin! Arsehole!' Seren shouted after him. She took a long drag of the next Lucky Strike she took from me. 'So, brother how art thou?' she asked.

I smiled and shrugged, 'what was all that with Lily?' I asked.

She shrugged, 'drunk'.

I waited for some elaboration. Nothing.

'How are you feeling?' she asked.

I was touched and surprised by her concern.

'Why do you ask?'

'I haven't talked to you for ages bro. And the last time I did, well you weren't too well.'

I had no recollection of this. She must have spotted my blank expression, 'At the hospital?'

Still nothing. She looked at me as if I had done something wrong.

'I don't remember any of it, sis. What happened?'

Silence. She thought carefully, then decided not to pursue the matter. 'What are you going to do?' she asked after another interminably long drag on her cigarette.

I looked blankly at her.

'About this,' she spread her arms to indicate the gwli, the pub, the village, the universe, life?

'What?'

'This. Fucking this.'

She was starting to get a little annoyed with me now. I don't know if she thought I was stupid, pretending to be stupid, or what. For all her front and seeming shallowness it really was difficult to work out what she was thinking.

I thought for a while, 'Nothing. I guess I'll just carry on with my work.'

'Work? You're a detective who has one case. Sorry. I mean you're a detective that used to have one case.'

'I still have that one case.' I said defensively. Then added 'technically'.

She took another cigarette from me, lit it from the nip of the old one then dropped the old one on the floor and squashed it. I did the same.

'You're a detective. Don't you want to find out who did it?' she asked.

'But I know who did it. You know who did it. Everyone knows who did it. Don't they?'

'So what are you going to do about it?'

I shrugged.

I could feel Seren's eyes boring into me. I didn't look up. She sighed and continued, 'I really liked Cai.'

'No you didn't.' I smiled.

'I really did. We were together when you were', slight pause, 'away.'

'You weren't.'

'I was.' She said this quietly.

'Together?'

'Together.'

'Together together?' I asked. This was hard for me to understand, obviously.

'Together. To fucking gether. Together'. This time she spoke a good deal louder.

I took a long drag of my cigarette, 'I didn't know that.'

Seren explained patiently and quietly, 'You were away, arsehole.'

'Who else knew?'

'Most people.' She paused. 'Mynydd Eimon hasn't changed you know. It's still the same small, sad, shitty little village. No secrets in this place.'

'So nothing at all has changed in a decade?' I asked.

'Nope', was the answer, 'No alarms and no surprises.'

Silence.

'You heard from dad at all?' I asked.

'Nope'.

'Mum?'

She looked hard at me, 'nope.'

She was starting to look angry again. I had always had this knack of winding her up. I had assumed it was because I was her annoying baby brother who used to follow her like a lost puppy for a dozen years. Now I think I was doing it deliberately. I decided to stop. I changed the subject, 'so what happened sis? What happened to me ten years ago?'

'How the fuck should I know. It's all your boys' club bollocks isn't it?'

I knew what she was talking about. I tried to steer the conversation away from that particular can of hot worms. She had a thing about me getting preferential treatment from our family. She reckoned it was because I had a dick. I think it's because I'm naturally charming and likable. I would never tell her that though.

22

'Where did they tell you I had gone?'

She looked at me as if I were an idiot, 'They wouldn't tell me anything would they? They never told me anything about mum, dad, or any fucking thing. I was hoping you would know something by now.' She stared hard at me.

'I don't. I was away, remember.'

'You knew, you little shit. You knew before you went away.' She said.

'I didn't. Honest sis. I had no idea it was going to happen'. I wasn't one hundred percent sure what I was pleading ignorance about but it seemed the best approach. I didn't know anything about my trip to America, I don't think. As to other stuff, boy's club stuff, I didn't know if I did or not. I couldn't remember those years at all. I didn't feel like I knew why my mother left, or I left, or where my father disappeared to. Did I?

'You didn't worry about me when you tried to kill yourself did you?' She waited two beats, then 'fuck you' she said. She dropped her cigarette, scrunched it with her foot and walked back into the pub. She had obviously been saving that line up for years. I sort of remembered, but thought it was a dream really. I hadn't been well. I remember hanging from the beam, but not why, or how I got there. I remember being cut down and put into the back of Dai Proper's van, coughing a lot. I remember bits and bobs about being in America for seven years but that all seemed like a long, long, long dream. Well, not a dream exactly. I knew it was real, sort of. But not. If you see what I mean? That was all. I remember nothing about the three years after that, or getting back here. It just sort of happened. This was how my head was recently - shot to bits.

On the positive side ten years away from Mynydd Eimon and it didn't look as if I'd have to work too hard to get up to speed with all the changes. I wandered back into the pub.

5 I Know Who Really Killed Him

I walked in to Jimmy Helms *"Gonna Make You an Offer You Can't Refuse"*, playing quite loudly. The room had become a good deal louder. The awed, respectful silence had lasted probably four cigarettes and two pints of Felinfoel. It was replaced with a loud murmur interspersed with shrill, low laughter and the occasional disbelievingly jovial, 'fuck off'.

I was deciding who I should sit by. I didn't feel like sitting by anyone. I was tired, had a headache and wanted to go home. It had been a testing few weeks for me. I looked around. On the old farts table Aunty Mary and Pedwar Penn were still talking down a spirited Lily. Seren and Amos were arguing on another table. I watched. I didn't like Amos very much. He looked like a boy who hadn't grown up. He was a boy trapped in a man's suit.

I contemplated leaving. It was a mistake. I shouldn't have contemplated - just left. I should have just left immediately. Lily approached me. She was as drunk as a new dropped calf. She tottered and staggered and laughed her way toward me. She was wearing a long frock with a lowish cut neckline. It was a funny beige colour. If I had to sum it up in a word, the word would be dowdy. It was something your aunt might wear that could be worn on any number of occasions. She was also smoking like a fourteen year old boy behind the bike sheds. Big puffs, exuberant gestures and a sense of 'she's going to regret this in the morning'. She tottered toward me on high heels. She clearly wasn't designed for them, nor them for her. It was all very bizarre. Lily was my absolutely ideal worker. She didn't cost me a penny. She was perfect. Physically she was pretty, well rounded and strong. She was mentally extremely strong, or incredibly stubborn (take your pick), as well. She was a brilliant secretary, ruthlessly efficient, obedient and very, very protective. She was however, utterly humourless. She was also not blessed, or burdened, with any shades of grey. She did what was asked – no less. Waiting for Lily to surprise you was as futile as waiting for a good simile to end this description.

'Hi boss.' She said. I had been her boss for a week or so now. She had appeared on the first day I'd opened the office. I had no idea who paid her. I didn't. Although I suspect it may have had something to do with Uncle Daniel. Lily never brought the subject up. I really liked her. However, just at this moment I wanted to be walking away from her.

'Lily', I acknowledged.

'I've been drinking', she told me redundantly, trying to talk, smoke and drink at the same time.' Cai's dead.' She announced.

'I know.' I said.

'I know who killed him.'

'So do I.'

'But I know who *really* killed him.'

'Well done, Lily. You'd make a fine detective.'

She smiled then frowned, 'the golf club killed him.'

'Yes, that's right. He was the professional and all that hard work playing golf, drinking and gambling finally got him. Well done Lily.'

She giggled, 'I'm bad Sammy, so bad.'

Then, to my delight, Uncle Daniel came to take me away.

'Sorry Lily.' I said, 'I need to go. See you later, if you're still with us.' I regret saying that now.

I breathed a sigh of relief as Daniel took me to the bar. I hate drunk people. They are so useless, like little, whinny, annoying, stupid drunken babies.

I walked with Uncle Daniel to the bar. I stepped back to allow him to buy me a drink. I looked at him. He hadn't changed at all. Daniel Llewellyn, solicitor and best friend to my father. He was the second in command. The consigliere. I called him my uncle, although he wasn't related by blood. I think it's a Welsh thing that the terms 'uncle' and 'aunty' don't necessarily mean blood relation. It's usually a term for someone your parents like who live not too far from you.

'Sam. What'll you have?'

'Whiskey please.'

'Large Four Roses for my favourite nephew, if you'd be so kind.' he commanded the barman. The normally slow, apathetic young barman served the drinks extremely quickly. Daniel turned back to me. He handed me the drink. We said cheers. He took a long drink of his wine and said, 'Sam. Sam. What are we going to do with you?'

I ignored this. It wasn't a question.

'Bad business with young Cai, eh?' He lit a fat cigar, 'Bad business.'

We were standing at the bar trying to have a sensible discussion in the middle of, what was basically now, an extremely crowded cattle market. The mooing didn't seem to bother him. I looked at him as he puffed on his cigar opulently. As I say this was the first time I'd talked to Daniel properly in years yet I remembered even now that Uncle Daniel frequently seemed to speak in statements. There was often no need to reply. He didn't expect it and he tended not to listen if you did. He was used to having his way in everything, even words. He studied my face.

'I can see traces of your father in you. I really can.'

There was a lot not being said. This was unusual for Daniel. I wondered should I help him. I decided that I wouldn't. He took another fat puff of his fat cigar, 'Now Sam I know you like all those old films so,' he paused for effect, 'I'm going to make you an offer you can't refuse.' Daniel smiled at his wit. He looked around. It was too crowded even for him now. He said, 'Samael. Walk with me.' He waddled off toward the door that led to gwli. I looked around, waited a few seconds and followed him.

6 Uncle Daniel Offers Me A Job

The gwli was clear. I was looking forward to this discussion. I kept telling myself to stay calm. 'Listen, listen', I repeated to myself. Daniel loved the sound of his own voice, his own importance. I just needed to listen. Let him talk too much and tell me the truth. But first I needed to talk and get something out of the way, 'You've got details of the will, I guess?'

'Very good. Very good,' Daniel smiled, 'very direct as always young Sam. I assume you want to know how much you will be left.'

'Not really. No. I'm not sure Cai had very much to leave. He is, sorry, he was, a poor golf club professional, drank a little, gambled a lot, lived in a room at the golf club. I'm pretty sure he's not likely to leave millions.' I paused, 'and what would I do with money anyway?'

'True. So very true. But Sam did you ever consider that he may leave you something even better than money?'

This wasn't really a question. I waited.

'Can you imagine what that would be Sam? Can you?' I waited. He truly treasured these moments waiting as he puffed excitedly on his cigar.

The little rotund git paused for dramatic purposes, 'His job Sam. His job.'

I spoke, 'Mynydd Eimon golf professional?'

'With all that comes with it. All the dividends, the benefits.'

'Really. I'm not interested Uncle Daniel, I've already got a job.'

'But this would be a real job. You would have killed for this job a few years ago.'

'Inappropriate.'

'Sorry. I'm sorry. But really Sam. Think about it. You could still

29

play at Philip Marlowe, or Taff Noir or whatever you call it. Come and join us at the club. What do you say?'

I ignored this. 'So when do we talk about my lost years?' I asked with no great expectation of getting an answer.

He laughed. 'Oh Sam. Samael my boy. We have an eternity for that. We need to talk about your current situation.'

'No thanks. Not until you tell me what's gone on with me in the past decade.'

He weighed up how serious I was. What could I do? I knew the only smidgen of power I had was the displeasure of my father. He knew that I knew this. He obviously decided that I was reaching the point where I may say something to my father.

'We decided you needed some leadership training.' He explained.

I was surprised. 'Who are we?'

'Well, your father really, and me.'

I waited hoping he would continue. He did.

'We were in 'the Lamb' one evening. Just talk, you know. You were, oh I don't know, about sixteen or so. You were becoming a pain in the arse as I remember. You were bored, I guess. You had no idea what you wanted to do next did you?'

He looked at me. I waited.

'So, we decided for you. No real, definite plan, but the start of an idea. We needed to give you some life skills training.'

'Couldn't you just have sent me to Harvard?' I asked.

Uncle Daniel laughed, 'Oh Sam you are a card. You truly are.' He took another huge puff on his cigar. 'Now where was I? Oh yes. So, he had just visited America and had heard great things. We all love golf. All angels love golf. So he thought, with your talents, it could work.'

I waited for the confirmation.

'We saw an opening. We found someone who had the same

birth time as you.'

'What a coincidence.' I said.

He ignored me, 'so we waited and worked, Amos helped with the, eh mechanics, and we shipped you off to America. It took a fair amount of planning I can tell you. Your mother wasn't too happy about it. But she came around in the end.' He paused, 'We waited for the right time and then we put you into the body of Bobby Jones.'

'You have got to be fucking kidding me.' I said. I was surprising more upset than I thought I would be. I sort of knew this transmutation, or whatever it was, had happened, but the confirmation still hurt. A lot.

He laughed. I looked at his fat smiling face and nearly punched him. For the ten days I'd been back I'd had dreams, nightmares about leaving my children, my wife, a life I had found. Love I had found and lived for seven whole years. I was in tears most nights imagining the faces of my children, my wife.

'I guess it's a bit, well, unorthodox. But it'll make a man of you, young Samael. It will be the making of you. As a leader. A leader of men. You mark my words.'

He started to move back to the door. I felt that I was being dismissed. 'Right Sam. That's enough for you to be thinking of now. Your father will answer all your questions when he returns.'

I stared at him.

He smiled, 'When will he return? No-one knows the day or hour. Not even the angels in heaven, but he will come like a thief in the night. Just joking Sam, Just joking. I really have no idea where he is now. China, maybe?'

'And my mother?'

'Oh come on Sam. You never, really, expected me to answer that one. Did you?' He opened the door and left me standing there.

Bobby Jones' Remembers

Atlanta, Georgia June 17th 1924

This was the date when I would finally marry my childhood sweetheart, Mary Rice Malone. The wedding was held at her parents' home. It was a real old-fashioned Southern wedding. The orchestra was playing, there was a tent out in the garden. Hundreds of people attended that evening. It was a great Georgian evening night. It was ridiculously cutesy.

I remember the wedding march across the lawn. There was the big moon, petals on the grass and as I saw Mary I was so close to tears. I was the happiest man alive, and yes, I know how trite and clicked that sounded but it was true. It was an amazing Atlanta evening and ... well, it was just perfect. It was a dream come true. This was only topped by the births of my three children, Clara Malone, Robert Tyre III and Mary Ellen. I loved and adored each of them in a different and special way. I know, I know, I know. Cliché on cliché on cliché - It doesn't mean it wasn't true though, does it?

7 Pedwar Penn

As I walked back into the bar the Harry Richman version of '*Putting on the Ritz*' started up. I wanted to cry. I took a deep breath and looked around. In the time it took me to walk from the gwli to here I had decided that I needed to be more proactive. I needed to take the initiative. I needed to work. Needed to find something to do. I had a paying client so I decided I would do a little detective work. Like all good detectives I went to the source. Fortunately, the source and the client were the same person, Aunty Mary.

She was still sat, buttoned up and morose at her table with Pedwar Penn and Lily. She had not moved an inch in the hours the reception was going on. I pulled up a chair next to Aunty Mary. I studied the three of them. Aunty Mary sat cradling her sweet sherry, staring and tutting at various people in the room. Lily looked like a sad faced clown with her mascara forming ridiculous black circles around her eyes. She was quiet now, almost soporific listening to Pedwar. If there's one thing guaranteed to calm anyone down, or put anyone to sleep, it's Pedwar Penn's voice. It seemed to be working a charm on a class full of adolescent schoolchildren. It seemed to be doing the job on Lily. He has a voice that could charm the suicides from the trees.

He soothed her, 'Lily, my flower, do relax my lovely. You're really going to be ill, you know. Come, sit down Lily.'

Pedwar Penn looked like a sad, slightly disturbed, cartoon, Welsh head teacher. He gave the impression of being the Welshest Welshman I had ever known. He was long, dark and gruff. He loved the sound of his own voice, which was just as well as, from memory, no-one else did. He was also a human thesaurian avalanche. Additionally, his sentences were generally so, so, so slow, so, so, so long, and so, so, so turgid, boring and drawn out. He was a half speed version of David Lloyd George. Surprisingly, given the fact that you needed the fortitude of Saint Monica to listen to him, he was the most impatient man I had ever met. It was like sitting on a volcano. A Welsh volcano, llosgfynydd Cymraeg. At school we called him Paroxysm Pedwar. I wish. We were never that well educated. We called him 'Powder Penn. Short for Gunpowder Penn. I know, it's sad isn't it? Although Aunty Mary had not moved the whole afternoon, as I looked around, she did.

'Lily, fy blodyn, let's keep you walking, shall we? You're really going to be ill, you know.' Aunty Mary had stood up and taken Lily's hand. She guided her to Daniel's table. I watched them go then turned to see and smell Powder Penn's oval face. He tried to disguise the ovalness with strands of hair and an unkempt, unruly moustache but it didn't work. If anything it emphasised the shape a little more. He also emanated a smell of smoke and Guinness.

He greeted me ridiculously loudly, 'Samael. Samael. How the devil are you?'

I gave a little Gallic shrug.

'Samael, you used to be a really, really good boy. Really good. Tremendous potential. Tremendous'. He said this in a very Welsh way emphasising the 'Tre'. 'Tremendous potential' he repeated. He sort of hypnotised me and I wanted to slip into my passive, comatose, hebetudinous mode. Then, I remembered giving myself a good talking to about this. 'Proactive, Sam, proactive' I whispered to myself and forced myself to talk, 'So, what was I like as a child?' I asked. Quickly trying to channel the assault. I had to bite my tongue not to add 'sir'.

'You always wanted to be in the movies, didn't you Sam? Or a detective?' He stopped to look at me carefully. He started again, 'Even better you really wanted to be a detective in the movies, didn't you?' He stopped. He started again, 'Yes, a real, gumshoe detective. What

34

happened to that?'

I looked at him with 'hilarious' in my eyes.

He laughed and shook as if it were the funniest thing in the world. It wasn't. He continued 'So young Samael. You're still asking lots and lots of questions are you?' he droned.

'I'm trying, but I'm not getting lots of answers.'

He stopped to think, then continued, 'So, Samael, tell me.' He paused, 'What is it that you want to know?'

I thought I'd just as well take a big punt, if I was going to take any punt at all, 'My sister says I tried to kill myself when I was sixteen. Why would I do that?'

'Why would anyone do that Samael?' he asked redundantly.

'Why did I do that?' I insisted. This may work. He was taken slightly off guard.

The headmaster slowly adopted the sitting praying mantis position with his hands folded in prayer and his chin resting on them, like an egg in a bizarre, avant-garde egg cup. 'You were unhappy' he eventually announced.

'I sort of worked that out, sir.'

'You got in with a bad crowd.'

'Who? Where?'

'At the golf club'

I didn't say anything.

He followed up with, 'Vernal Section'.

I didn't say anything.

'Youth, glaslanc, adulescentia, junior' he translated.

He closed his eyes and continued, 'When I was a windy boy and a bit and the black spit of the chapel fold.'

I managed to head him off that particular pass with a question I had wondered about all my life, 'Why is golf so important in Mynydd

Eimon?'

'Ah, Samael. Golf is perfect – par, one under, eagle, handicaps. It's all maths. Numbers – 6, 13, 17, 18.'

I didn't say anything.

'Maths is the devil in detail.' He added.

I didn't say anything again.

'As Saint Augustine said, 'the good Christian should beware of mathematicians. Mathematicians have made a covenant with the devil to darken the spirit and to confine man in the bonds of Hell.'

I continued not to say anything.

Penn continued 'We love golf – it's beautiful, pure, perfect.'

I didn't say anything, yet again and pretended to look bored.

He opened his eyes, stopped and I saw an instant of panic in his eyes as he replayed the past 30 seconds wondering if he had said too much. He concluded that he hadn't, but realised he was close to actually saying something useful so he stopped. I'd worked all this out in point six of a second, of course. I could have been wrong, but in my business you learn to trust your instincts. I knew I had the measure of Mr Penn so I relaxed and waited for my opportunity.

We stared at each other looking for weaknesses.

He settled back and thought deeply. He weighed up a number of factors – what he could say, what he couldn't, how much to lie, how much truth to tell. He made his decision, chose his script and delivered his homily;

'Up until the time you were sixteen you were the perfect child'.

'Perfect?' I interjected.

'You were a lovely child – bright, inquisitive, a bit cheeky but plenty of charm. Enough charm to get away with it.......... before you were sixteen. Then you became a loner, a recluse, an outsider if you will. You went off the rails.'

Mr Penn had this wonderful over the top Welsh way of making everything sound like a very, very intriguing shopping list. All style. No substance.

'You were still a remarkable golfer. A quite remarkable golfer but a charmless person on the golf course. You played and beat practically all the golfers in that year. Everyone except Cai. No-one beat him. You remember? No, of course you don't. But you were extraordinary. You were the youngest winner of the junior medal at sixteen, junior captain at sixteen, winner of the senior Champion Putter at sixteen...'

I feigned boredom and remarked, 'Sixteen seems to be coming up a lot.'

'I'm trying to tell you something,' he practically screamed at me.

'What exactly are you trying to tell me.... sir?'

He was practically shaking, 'It was you or Cai. You knew that. Fuck you.'

And with that he stormed off. It had always been easy to wind Mr Penn up. He was so highly strung. I stopped and thought. I wondered if this was going the right way for me. Was I making any headway? I wasn't sure, but I knew I felt a little better, now. Pathetic really. I glanced at my watch. It was now almost nine o'clock. Should I stay or should I go now? I'd had enough really. Then Aunty Mary and Lily came back. Well Lily came about ten feet from me, waved a sorry goodbye and left. Aunty Mary sat next to me.

'How's Lily now?' I asked.

'Troubled.'

I started to formulate a question but nothing came out.

'I suppose this would be the time I tell you about killing Cai, cariad.' Aunty Mary said.

8 Flashback Sunday July 9th 1933

'Aunty Mary! Aunty Mary!' he called as he pushed open the front door and walked along the passageway. He looked into the front room on his right at the perfectly clean armchairs and sofa and once again cursed himself for wasting five seconds of his life looking for Mary in a room that was never used except for Sundays or visitors. He closed the door quietly and listened.

He heard a noise from upstairs as Mary Ap Gwelym shuffled across the bedroom toward the stairs. He walked back through the passageway to the foot of the stairs, 'Aunty Mary. Come down now. I've got something to tell you.....some news.'

She left her duster on the dressing table and moved gingerly down the stairs.

'Henaint ni ddaw ei hunan. Old age doesn't come by itself.' she muttered to herself.

Slowly, slowly she descended, tentatively placing her foot on the mat at the foot of the stairs and closed the open front door.

'What's all this palaver cariad?' she asked.

'I just came to tell you about the Ystrad Cup. I was second. I know I usually win but Sam won it. He played really well. I'm so pleased for him. So glad he's back... A bit of a surprise that?' he beamed.

Mary hobbled into the front room.

'I was told to expect that', she announced.

'Who said that', he asked.

'Oh we talk you know. We talk us girls. Fy blodau and me. We talk.' She muttered to herself.

He followed her into the room, 'Great to have Sam back though isn't it? I really missed him. Great isn't it?'

38

'Could you pass me my bag from that drawer please? It's in the dresser there.' She pointed to a drawer in the large Welsh dresser.

Cai got the bag from the drawer, and handed it to her.

'Thank you. Diaown' answered Mary. She opened the bag, reached in, pulled out an army revolver and fired three shots into his heart.

9 Father Barry

I listened to Aunty Mary's story. She told it absolutely unemotionally. She waited patiently for follow up questions. I didn't really want to ask anything. I wanted to go home. Then I remembered that I should be professional. Professional detectives asked professional questions.

'Why Aunty Mary? Why?'

'Because he was second, wasn't he? He wasn't first. If he had been first it would have been OK? There can only be one winner.'

'But I was first. What if I'd been second?'

'But you were first, cariad. We knew you'd be first.'

'What happened to the body?'

'Oh Daniel took care of that.'

'And the police?'

She looked blankly at me. 'Why would the police be involved?'

'Sorry,' I muttered. In all my life in Mynydd Eimon I had never seen a policeman or woman. I'd seen them on television. I'd seen them in America, but never live in Mynydd Eimon. Why would a small village in Wales need to bother with the police? I couldn't really think of any more questions, but I asked one just the same, 'But why?'

She treated me and my question with the disdain it deserved.

I saw Father Barry and Amos approaching. Aunty Mary stood up and moved to Daniel's table. I had the feeling that the whole evening was choreographed precisely. First Seren, then Daniel. Then Pedwar, then Aunty Mary. Now this pair. However, Amos walked straight past and out of the door. It was obviously not time for him. Just yet. I felt quite fed up with being manipulated and used. Not that I was getting paranoid or anything. It all seems just a little silly to me. I crushed my cigarette into the ashtray. There's the story I've been told regarding poker. When you play poker you're always looking for the fish, the patsy, the sucker, the easy money. If you're in a poker game, and after you've been playing for twenty minutes and you still haven't identified the fish, then leave. You're the fish. I'm pretty sure I was the fish, the patsy in Mynydd Eimon. It wasn't that I was not very good at the game. It was the fact that I didn't know what game we were playing. I breathed. I counted to ten, in Welsh. I thought, 'What choice do I have? And anyway what else was there to do in Mynydd Eimon on a Friday night? Or any night for that matter.'

Father Barry was sitting next to me. He looked worse than he had looked a few hours ago. He looked a little like a skinny version of Rasputin. He had the beads, and the eyes. He stared at me with the eyes. If Pedwar could put you to sleep then Barry could keep you awake at night.

'Samael. Samael. Samael.' He said, oleaginously. He seemed to encapsulate the very essence of a snake oil salesman.

'Father. Father. Father.' I couldn't stop myself replying.

He sat opposite me with a large glass of whiskey.

'Tell me about Mary, Barry. Father Barry. Tell me about Mary.'

'A troubled soul.'

'Really – how so?'

'She's never really been one of us.'

'Us?'

'How could she,' he mused. He feigned thinking, pretending that this little speech wasn't prepared, 'She's a servant, not a martyr, a watcher not a witness. She's just a pawn. She's not important.'

I must have looked especially confused. He tried to clarify.

'She's not one of us.' He repeated emphasising each word. 'She's a pawn. Who knows who moved her?'

'Moved her?' I asked.

'Like a chess piece'. He demonstrated, needlessly I thought, how to move something. In this case an ashtray. I looked in wonder and awe at him.

I tried another tack, 'She wants you to look after her soul.'

He laughed, 'Why?'

I laughed, 'Because she's killed someone. She committed a mortal sin, hasn't she?'

'But she's not really one of us.' He explained patiently.

'Was Cai?'

'Well, yes', he paused, 'and no.' He clarified, 'He isn't now.'

I had had enough of this particular line of questioning. I had the sense that Father Barry was working to some weird kind of script. The others had their own script and they carried it out, pretty well, but as with Pedwar there was some opportunity to tilt them a little bit. Barry was different. He was, well, odd. In an odd way. How can you tilt someone who is already tilted? I couldn't goad him as I had with Pedwar. I'd need to find some emotional button somewhere to engineer a mistake. It was cat and mouse. It was an English idiom dating back to 1675 that means 'a contrived action involving constant pursuit, near captures, and repeated escapes. It was like two tiny bantamweights circling each other, each afraid of upsetting the other, but needing to. I was starting to over-think this, wasn't I? However, I decide to jab at a more general question in the hope that this would be something off-script for him.

'Why are we so special, Father Barry?' I fished.

'Because we have certain powers, of course'.

'Such as?'

He explained it to me, as a patient person would do to a small, slightly stupid, child. 'We can mess with time a little.'

'Really?' I actually did stroke my chin.

42

He had another go, 'how old are you, Sam?'

'Well I was sixteen when I left. Apparently I left for seven years so...'

He stopped me. 'Oh Samael, Samael, Samael. Not mathematics. I abhor mathematics. Life isn't mathematics. Tell me. What year do you think it is?'

I had some ideas sloshing around in my head. Mathematically it should be 1931 give or take for some months and allowances for my memory. But it wasn't. I knew it was 1933. I wasn't feeling confident about my memory. Had I left at sixteen? Had I come back in 1930? Was I gone for seven years? I must have looked confused. This was literally, literally giving me a headache.

Father Barry reassured me, 'Time is just a number Sam. You have your head full of books, films, television from the 1940s, 50s, 60s, 70s, 80s, 90s, 2000s. Doesn't that seem strange?'

It didn't. But it should have, now that I thought about it. I wanted to talk about this more but Father Barry shuffled in his seat and I realised I only had a few more minutes left before my audience with the father was concluded. I conceded this round to Barry. For my final, knockout-attempted punch, I put all my proverbial eggs in one proverbial parental basket.

'Tell me about my mother, Father Barry?'

'Ah!' he pressed his fingers together. I had caught him off guard. He defended, 'Why now?'

'I was told never to answer a question with a question, weren't you?'

'I was, but why now?'

'It's time.'

'It's time' he repeated slowly. He reflected, and sighed. 'I suppose you're right - it is time. Tell me Samael what do you remember of her?'

He was fighting more cleverly than I remembered. His scraggled appearance hid a lifetime of experienced techniques for dealing with difficult questions, as I guess all priests have done, and will do in the future. In danger of mixing my sporting metaphors here I'd have to say that he batted it back to me. Thinking quickly, I returned it, 'there you go again. I remember nothing after the age of about sixteen. You know this.' I said emotionally, half-pretending to be upset.

Surprisingly he admitted something, 'she disappeared around the same time as you did. Just left one winter evening and left you and your sister alone in the house. She has never returned.'

'Or her body has never been found', I interjected with a theory of my own.

'Yes.' He said slowly. Pause, 'It's a mystery.'

I realised I had seen some light at the end of the tunnel, the Promised Land, the thing with feathers. But now he had slammed it shut. God, even my metaphors were falling at the first hurdle.

In desperation I resorted to the truth. I was getting more than a little upset as I asked, 'Father, I know that this is true. But tell me Father. What was she like? Tell me something about her. Anything.'

'She was perfect.'

This came as something of a shock to me as I'd never heard anything of her character. The few people I'd tried to talk to since my return had faked sympathy and then quickly changed the subject at the mention of my mother.

'Perhaps too perfect' he continued enigmatically.

'No-one is too perfect.'

'Perhaps you're right,' he agreed.

This was getting nowhere. I sort of lost it at this point.

Through gritted teeth I asked, 'And you father.....what's your story?'

He was getting really bored now. 'You still ask lots of questions Samael, don't you?'

'Still?'

'Yes. You were always in trouble for asking lots of questions. Too many questions.'

I had had enough of this enigmatic nonsense. I had stopped but Barry continued, 'I'm a priest Samael. I know everything.'

'Do you know where all the bodies are buried Father?'

He smiled for the first time. 'Most of them.' He admitted. Then he thought for a while longer, as if checking, 'Most of them.'

He stood up and walked away.

I stood up and left. I had had a gutsful.

10 The Ruins

After the worst interview since Herod met with John the Baptist, I felt I
had lost by two falls and one submission to nil. I left the pub and
decided to spend some time at the old ruins before I went home. I
needed to think carefully. I used to go to the ruins when I was young,
regularly. I always did this as a boy. I'm not sure what they were ruins
of, to tell the truth - a monastery, a roman settlement, ancient Celt's
burial ground? No-one in the village seemed to know either. It felt
peaceful though. I walked through what I assumed was the entrance
and sat on a pile of stones in the dead centre of the ruins. I wondered
how I could remember so much about this place yet only have vague
feelings and impressions of the last few years. I had carried out some
research recently and I had concluded that I probably had some sort of
amnesia. One particular theory suggested that, 'disorientation was a
hysterical reaction motivated by a desire to return home.' Which was a
little ambiguous for me. I agreed with the disorientation part. That was
fairly constant for me at present. I felt 'so, so' about the hysterical
reaction, but struggled with my definition of home. Was home Mynydd
Eimon, or Atlanta? Perhaps it was this inability to find a home that was
responsible for the hysteria. Maybe, and here's a novel thought, it wasn't
me who was suffering from hysteria, but everyone else. There had been
many recorded cases of mass hysteria. I read about one instance of
mass hysteria, the dancing plague of Strasbourg in 1518. Apparently in
July of 1518 one woman, Frau Troffea, started dancing over 400 people
started dancing in the streets. This followed one person dancing non-
stop in the streets. Others followed over the next days and weeks until
there were over four hundred dancing a month or so later. The people
danced until they dropped dead from exhaustion or starvation. Now, I'm

not suggesting something as strange as that is happening in Mynydd Eimon but maybe I'm the only one not dancing. What if I'm normal and everyone else is crazy? It makes you think, doesn't it? Pondering thoughts like this I sat and smoked. Three cigarettes later I hadn't resolved anything so I stood up to move. I felt as if I had danced for weeks.

From the corner of my eye I noticed something on my left that shouldn't have been there. It was a mound, dark and grey. It was there near the wall. It shouldn't have been there. It shouldn't have been a mound there at all, actually. I walked toward it. A few yards away I could see that it was a body lying face down just in front of a small stone wall. I moved closer. I turned it over. Its head was covered with blood. It had Lily's features. There were bruises all over the bare arms and face. She looked smaller somehow. I didn't feel sympathy or upset. I felt confused, and to be absolutely truthful, selfish. How will this affect me? What was I supposed to do in a situation like this? Should I know? Should I check for fingerprints or something? How long do I need to leave it before I recruit a new secretary? Murder is supposed to be my business but to be honest this was the first dead body I'd ever seen. I had a copy of 'things to do at a homicide scene' somewhere. I decided that it would be useful to have on me at all times, in Mynydd Eimon at least.

I remembered something I had read in bold type, from somewhere, 'Don't move the body'. On the plus side, I wasn't panicking. I just totally froze. Eventually I realised that could move. So I did. I stayed clear of the body, just looking at some footprints and picking up a cigarette butt I had found. I reminded myself to find out all the procedures for all these types of situations tomorrow. But for now - what the hell should I do?

I wondered who would be the best person to see in a situation like this. I decided I needed to move. I would have to leave Lily alone, which seemed disrespectful somehow, but I thought it was something I needed to do. Then I realised that I probably should see a doctor. Unfortunately the only doctor I knew was not the most competent. Still, 'needs must' as my father used to say and I left the ruins to find Dr Craddoc.

11 Taking Charge

He didn't seem to know what to do either. 'Um, don't move the body?' he suggested.

I was at the home of Amos Caddoc. Doctor. He was sitting on an armchair cwtching a glass of whiskey. The armchair looked too big on him. He had obviously come straight from the reception at the Lamb, to his house and didn't seem to have had a break in his drinking. When you saw him drinking you had the feeling that you should take the glass away from him. He didn't look remotely old enough to drink, or smoke. He was doing both. He had obviously been drinking solidly for the best part of eight hours though, and it didn't seem to have affected him in the slightest. He had taken his jacket off. He still had his tie on though. He looked like a neat schoolboy sitting in an armchair slightly too big for him. Which in a way, emotionally, was true. He was as competent drunk as I remember him being competent sober.

'What did you do a few days ago when Cai died?' I asked.

He thought carefully, 'Your uncle sorted it all out.'

'Right.' I said. I took charge. 'Sis could you come with me back to Lily. Amos, go and find Daniel.' It seemed the best use of people's skills.

Seren was sitting next to me on the big, elegant sofa. I had woken her up. On my trip from the ruins to here I had passed her house. I needed my big sister to help me. I had knocked loudly on the door. She hadn't taken long to open it and tell me off for being so fucking loud. She informed me that she had been in bed fast asleep and didn't need me to disturb her. I must have looked pretty terrible at that point because once she looked properly at me she changed. She became my big sister again. I went into her house and sat quietly while she got ready to come with me. I noticed a few things whilst I was waiting the four minutes it took her. I'd love to say I found mud on her shoes and blood on her coat, but I didn't. I looked though. I did find a photo of my sister and Cai on a beach. I also found a love letter from Cai to her. These were hidden in her jewellery box, in the place she always thought she kept things she didn't want me to see. When she appeared she was wearing trousers and a new coat that was a good deal more functional for the task in hand.

Back to Amos' house. After my assertive instructions I waited for people to leap into action. I stood back and watched as Amos had another sip of his whiskey. Seren looked at me from the sofa in a way that seemed, to me at least, to suggest she was impressed that I had grown up, and become so forceful. Then she stood up.

'Sam, you go home. Leave all this to me. Amos, get to fucking bed.'

'Better.' I said, 'I'm coming with you though sis.' I insisted.

'If you like but there's going to be a lot of blood and you don't like that do you?'

'I don't.' Chipped in Amos.

I looked at him, then at Seren, 'I'm coming,' and as an afterthought, 'It'll be good experience for me. You know, detective - wise.'

She sighed. Amos went to bed and me and my sister left.

12 Murder Clean Up

My sister and I went back to the ruins. She was calm and purposeful. She was in control. She was wrapped up warm with a matching grey coat and scarf, probably a present. It was the type of things people in love buy for each other. It looked nice as well. I remembered something now. I remembered the night our mother disappeared (great title for a book that). Seren was in control just like she had been all those years ago the night our mother disappeared. That evening she led me by the hand, literally, and took me to Aunty Mary's house. She knocked on the door, hard, as I recall and when Aunty Mary appeared had thrust me at her. 'Look after him,' she had instructed Aunty Mary.

Aunty Mary had taken me, 'Seren, angel, where are you going?'

'Golf club,' Seren announced and then turned and ran along Alma Road toward Mountain Road and the club. It was cold, as I recall. I don't remember anything after that.

It was cold now but I was wrapped up and seemed to be doing all right, considering it was my first dead body.

'Don't worry. You're doing all right,' Seren said, 'considering...'

'I know. I know.'

We neared the scene of the crime. I fumbled in my pocket and brought out the article I had been thinking about. It was not called 'things to do at a homicide scene'. It was 'a checklist for a homicide investigation'. I started reading it. Most of it seemed irrelevant for Mynydd Eimon, but you've got to try to do the right thing haven't you? Lily had rushed on to examine the body. I was reading my checklist intently as I moved towards Lily's body.

'Looks like she was hit with a blunt instrument.' Seren deduced.

I frantically read through my checklist to see how she had

worked that out.

'Cuts and bruises on her head.' she explained.

'I see,' I remarked, looking at the cuts and bruises carefully. 'Um', I said wisely. Seren wandered off somewhere. Looking for clues no doubt. Something perhaps I should be doing. I examined Lily more thoroughly. I examined the cuts on her head. They were quite large and there was a large bump coming up on the back of her head. I saw some strands of wool stuck to the blood that covered her hair and neck. Her hair was red and matted with blood. It looked to be congealed which should have told me how long ago she had been killed. It didn't tell me anything. I put the strands of wool in my handkerchief, folded it and put it carefully in my pocket. The checklist suggested that the investigator enter the scene by the route least likely to disturb the evidence and then leave everything exactly as it was. It was too late for that, Seren had trampled over everything, picking up bits of rock, cigarette ends, tin cans. I bent down and looked at the cigarette butts. I stood up as I realised that I had missed something from my checklist. Apparently we had to check the victim for signs of life.

I called to my sister and conveyed it to her. She wandered back and looked at Lily, 'She looks dead enough to me,' was her professional medical response.

'She does, doesn't she?' I concurred. I wasn't that keen on putting my index finger and middle finger on her carotid artery what with all the blood and everything. I was hoping that Amos, or someone, would do that later. With him being a doctor and all it seemed that this should be his area of expertise. Anyway, I thought I'd leave that one.

My checklist demanded that if the victim was alive I should ask pertinent questions. It gave an example, 'Who did this to you?' This would be followed by questions describing the assailant, e.g. male, female, race, height, weight. I also had to 'establish the fact that the victim knows they are dying'. I wasn't much looking forward to that particular conversation. How would you know anyway? I read further down the list and decide that it really wasn't appropriate for this murder. It was a bit too detailed, really. My sister obviously felt the same as she was standing next to Lily and had open a pack of cigarettes and was smoking a Chesterfield. She poked one in my direction. I accepted and we both stared down at Lily.

I looked at the ground. It was still pretty wet. I saw my footprints around the body and Lily's, but no-one else's. This struck me as a little strange. What type of person doesn't leave footprints? In Mynydd Eimon there would be more than most, I suspected, but it was an area I needed to explore.

We smoked in silence for a few minutes. I was thinking, not about the death of Lily, but about how difficult it was going to be to find a new secretary. I had a lot of practical things on my mind at the moment. I barely knew Lily but I worried about myself that all I thought of this murder was that it was an inconvenience. Maybe it was because I'd lost so many people recently that I had become numb. Well, this was my justification anyway. I looked over at my sister. She looked thoughtful too. I had no idea what was going on in her mind. We had been really close once. But now? Today I had glimpsed the occasional moments when I felt close but there as so much going on with her and so much history I had missed that I wondered if we would ever be truly close again. I wanted to. I really did, but there was something dark inside Seren. During the past day I had seen glimpses of that as well. It must have been there when we were growing up, but hey, she was my kid sister and as we were evolving she was my hero, my sis, my Seren.

Daniel Llewellyn arrived noisily. I have no idea who told him. He was in the front of a van alongside Dai Proper and Dai Copy. He walked over to Lily's body and I swear I saw him hold back a tear. He lifted her up and laid her on a flat rock nearby that looked like some primitive altar.

'We shouldn't move the body,' I said.

He stared at me blankly. He looked at her face carefully, looking for clues I guess. I thought of asking him where he was at the time of the murder, but it seemed a little corny and callous, and I doubt he would have told me the truth anyway. So I just observed carefully that was on the list too. Daniel was holding her and touching her. Not inappropriately, just examining and disturbing the evidence. I realised he was looking for clues as well. Christ is everyone in Mynydd Eimon a wannabe detective?

After a few minutes Uncle Daniel looked across at Dai Copy and nodded. Dai Copy moved towards Lily's body, and carried it to the van. Daniel looked at me and Seren and then went back to the van. Dai Proper drove all three of them into the night.

Seren walked away without a look or a word. I stayed for a while and removed all my selfish thoughts. I took a deep breath. I turned into a proper detective and thought hard about the past hour or so and asked myself a lot of questions. Why had Lily been killed? I needed to find out more about her. Why she had been assigned to keep an eye on me? Who paid her? I assumed it was Daniel but I needed to be sure. Why had Daniel looked at Lily like that? He seemed to almost care about someone? And my sister. Why was she so keen to get involved? Why had she picked up the Chesterfield cigarette butts near Lily's body and put them in her coat pocket surreptitiously? Amos was a wimp, yes but as the doctor he should have been, at least, a little interested in a dead body? Even if it were just for professional experience, or curiosity, like me? Who was running the golf club? Why had everyone trotted out their little speeches at the wedding like a child's school play? What the fuck was going on?

I was getting a real bad headache now.

THE TEACHER'S TALE

I ~~was~~ am the clever one. I only wanted to help. I wanted the quest for knowledge. He didn't want to. He rationed knowledge like rice in a famine. We all had our skills, our specialities. But it wasn't enough for me. I had a thirst, a hunger, for knowledge, you see. You could say that I was the one who started the unease, disquiet, trafferth - The Troubles. It was all down to the innovation of writing. For eons we were happy. There were factions, of course. But these cabals appeared and disappeared. We argued, of course we did. We are strong minded individuals, but nothing serious. Then it did start becoming serious. I decided to record everything. Well, decided to record certain things. I began to chronicle tales and stories and thoughts and deeds. It was a new toy. It was amazing. But, not everyone wanted their actions to be recorded. It was the start of the end. I taught others and we wrote, collected, catalogued and recorded. It became an obsession. It consumed us, I get that. It was a quest for the Truth. The objective, definitive truth. They hated it. He hated it. 'Why waste your time on documenting when you could be doing so much more to honour me.' We drifted apart into two tribes. Disharmony and distrust was always in the air after that. The finale was a long time coming - a series of crescendos - slowly, slowly, slowly, building. Slowly. Slowly. Simmering like a great cauldron of cawl. One day it inevitably boiled over. I had started to write a history. The history. Exact. Honest. The Truth. The History. He didn't like it. He forbade it. He destroyed it. Forbade free speech. That's when the Troubles began. And, well you know the rest.... 'Then war broke out in heaven' ... blah, blah, blah.

Ironically after The Troubles He became a great fan of it, the writing I mean, and ... well. They learnt quickly the value of the pen.

The usefulness of propaganda and ....'To the victor the spoils' and 'History is written by the winners' and so on and so forth.

Anyway. When the Troubles eventually ended (and it wasn't as cut and dried and one sided as they record, but 'History is written by winners..'), there were two hundred of us. We came here - earth, Wales, Mynydd Eimon. As the teacher I looked after our offspring and the children. I nurtured them. Most of our faction had little care for their progeny - they spread - they disappeared. They went out into the world and became part of the fabric - sleepers not watchers - hibernators. Five of us chose to stay. I was the fourth to be mentioned.

SATURDAY JULY 15th 1933

13 New Day

*Sky-red – blood red – falling – hit ground hard – not too hard –
office - golf club – red carpet – books and books and books - grey safe –
easy money – alone – Cai presence outside – falling – vultures –
watching – goading – sneering – flying and falling – flying and falling –
'destroy the ungodly' - angels – mother – Mary – stick – gopher wood –
battered old goose-necked putter – well done son - 'consummate
gentleman' - Bobby 'greatest ever' – Amy - One day - soon - Mary –
Molly – Malone – cockles and muscles alive alive-o – her ghost wheels
her barrow through the streets – 'Sam' - 'Wake up' – Run Sam run –
'Who built the ark, no-one, no-one. Who built the ark, brother? No-one
built the ark'– 'Wake up' - Bob – Mary – Sam*

I woke up at 5 o'clock, as usual, with a blinding headache and a half-
remembered dream. This was not unusual. For as long as I could
remember I had been living somewhere between sleep, memory and
reality. I wasn't sure what was real or not real anymore. OK that is a sort
of cliché, but cliché or not it did seem to sum up what I'm going
through.

I had a feeling of loss and confusion from the dream. Nothing
unusual there but in this particular dream I also had the sense of
exhilaration, of winning. It tapped into some memory of myself as a
success. I dressed and wandered up to the golf course. I felt that I had
to do this. I went into the unlocked locker room and put on my shoes
and picked up my golf bag. It felt good.

It was cold, misty and foggy. I could just make out the flag on
the first green from the tee 400 yards or so away. I hit 2 smooth 5 irons
to the green and holed a 6 feet putt for a birdie. The feeling of

exhilaration echoed the dream, as I knew it would.

I walked around the course slowly and played as if back in the dream. I was 4 under when I reached the clubhouse again after the first 9 holes. I stopped and wandered back down the hill. It was all starting to come into focus now. The good as well as the bad.

Flashback Saturday July 8th 1933

The sepia-toned Lamb was busy. People were talking, happy, being noisy, being annoying. In one corner there was an intense game of crib and don with a combined age of over three centuries for the four participants. The other corner a similarly aged group were playing 'devil amongst the tailors'. These were the highlights of the entertainment scene in Mynydd Eimon. This was entertainment in its loosest, most pathetic, most geriatric sense.

I looked around but even with my eyes shut and even with *my* memory I could tell where everyone would be sitting. There hadn't been a new face in the pub for as long as I could remember. The only progression had been boys turning fifteen and paying someone to buy their first timid, illegal, drinks in the back bar egged on by their experienced, worldly sixteen year old friends. At sixteen they progressed to their first communion at the bar. What a day that was for the parents and congregation. The invited guests, new suits, gifts, Father Barry saying a few words before serving the victim with Guinness and crisps. I'm joking. It wasn't always like that. Or rather it hadn't been like that for a while. I noticed now how few sixteen year olds there were. My return must have plunged the average age of the pub congregation to below three score and ten for the first time in ten years. However old I was?

I sat with my back to the wall, facing the door that led to the small dark room. I had read somewhere that this is what private eyes did, or was that secret agents, or gunmen? Whoever I was that had invented the process seemed to have hit on a great idea. Although I suspect it was also a traditional, powerful Feng Shui position. I sat and waited. This, waiting, wasn't something I did well. Which was curious in a way as one of the few job-related skills required for a good private detective was patience. Still, who said I was any good. I was waiting for the meeting in the back room to finish. This was a Saturday and every Saturday there was a meeting for the 'Friends of Mynydd Eimon'. No-one was really sure what the 'Friends of Mynydd Eimon' did. It was assumed they were a hard working charitable organisation with the sole purpose of helping the community of Mynydd Eimon. However, they never organised charitable events, never held raffles, dances, coffee mornings, bingo or whist drives. They did seem to meet regularly though.

I had been in the pub when they arrived; priest, headmaster, doctor, solicitor, golf club lackeys all and inevitably, Aunty Mary. I bought myself a drink, sat on my own and waited. I didn't know what I was waiting for, but I had the feeling something was brewing. I could hear noise from the small room, fairly heated arguments and the occasional forced laugh. I had the feeling they were rehearsing a play - although this may well be a case of me reframing this in the light of recent experiences. I would have tried to get closer but noticed the twins, Dai Proper and Dai Copy at the door. They were not exactly keeping guard but not exactly leaving the doorway clear for people to pass either. It was a very contrived chat they were having and they stared at me a great many times like they were livestock guardian dogs such as a Carpathian Shepherd Dog displaying the key qualities of trustworthiness, attentiveness and protectiveness, with the added bonus of implied violence.

Cai arrived, saw me, ordered a pint for himself and a whiskey for me. Now I could confirm that he still wasn't dead - at that time. He looked alive. He looked exactly like a golf pro should look – blonde, tanned (amazingly as he had lived all his life in a small, dark, valley in Wales), tall and athletic. Healthy. He looked annoyingly healthy and very much alive.

'You're not dead?' I checked as he sat down.

'No. Not yet.' He joked.

I hadn't talked at any length to Cai for over a decade I imagine. He had been a few years older than me. We had become best friends when I was around sixteen. We'd been inseparable for a year or so. Initially it was golf that gave us a common interest. As we became closer we found we had more in common. We used to go everywhere together, sharing everything, apparently. My recall of our time, whilst pretty decent, had large holes in it.

'I hear you've been busy with Aunty Mary?' he remarked sipping at his drink.

'I don't think I found out anything interesting.' I said.

'What do you want to know?' he asked

'Anything. Everything. Tell me about me.' I said, then realised that this sounded incredibly egotistic, or was it egoistic?

In the next fifteen minutes Cai told me everything he wanted to tell me about me. How I was a smashing friend - bit of a loner - terrific at golf - got in with a bad lot - Vernal Section - went off the rails a little - mother ran away from home and I had some sort of a breakdown - went away and returned a few months ago, blah, blah, blah.

'Where did I go?' I asked

'Away.'

'Away where?' I asked politely

'Abroad I think'

'England?'

'No, proper abroad – America.'

'Doesn't anyone know exactly where I went?'

'Daniel I expect'

'I see'. I said. I didn't really.

I casually brought up the subject of Cai's father, 'what happened to your father, Cai?'

'What do you mean?'

'Well – did he die? Did he go abroad?'

'I really don't know and I'm not sure I want to talk about it.'

I nodded. 'So what do you remember about him?' I continued

'Nothing really. I never saw him. Or my mother. I was raised by Aunty Mary. I asked, of course but no-one would ever tell me. There were rumours, teasings in school about him being dead. Killed by your father even. Stabbed apparently. But I didn't believe it. I just don't know.'

'Did it upset you?' I asked.

'Not really. I remember going home in tears to Aunty Mary and she told me not to be so ridiculous. She made a joke and said Uncle Sam would never use his hand, he'd use a gun – it would be easier. It made me laugh.'

I looked at Cai carefully. He was laughing. Weird.

'Did you know who your father was?' I asked.

'No. I never ever found out.' He was silent for some time. I thought he was thinking about who is father was but apparently not. 'So you really don't remember me at all? Not even when we were in school together?' Cai asked somewhat sorrowfully.

'Nope. Nothing.' I lied.

I remember he was really, really good at golf. He always used to beat me. I hated that. I did remember some things. I know we spent a lot of time together, but I don't know why. I knew vividly that I disliked Cai immensely. I'm not sure exactly why but I knew he had hurt me some time in the past. Not in any emotional, namby pamby sense but in a painful, cruel torturing way. I didn't know how, when or where but apart from those minor details I knew it with deep, total certainty. I

64

hated him for it. Something bad had happened to me and I knew Cai was involved.

'Same again?' I asked cheerfully as I got up and went to the bar.

'You're trying to get me drunk before tomorrow', said Cai.

'Not you. Me.' I thought.

15 Deja Vu, All Over Again

I opened the door of my Balaclava Road office at my usual time, nine o'clock precisely. I liked things to be right. I like things to be where they should be. I didn't have a long commute to the office so had no excuse to be late, not that I had a boss to answer to anyway. I lived above my office and had followed my usual routine. I had left my house ten minutes ago, I had left my house ten minutes ago, walked along Alma Road and Malakoff Street where I had picked up two packets of Lucky Strikes at Mrs Evans' corner shop. I returned on the same route to my office. I smiled at the exquisite lettering on the door of the office, "Samael K. Watcher ... Investigations". I didn't have a middle name but thought the 'K' added a touch of class. I passed through the waiting room where Lily, my former receptionist sat between nine thirty and five, less the hour I gave her for lunch, which she had never taken. 'Waiting room' was perhaps too grand a phrase for what was essentially a tiny front room in a mining terraced house hidden deep in a Welsh valley. More a holding pen. The pen had a desk with a phone. It was functional. The desk was old, solid and grey. Uncle Daniel had found it somewhere and someone had delivered it. It was exactly to my specification. I wasn't particularly creative when it came to interior design but I knew what I like. Even a minimalist interior design would have added a few more features to the room.

I opened the door of my inner office. I stepped inside. As I say I like things to be just so and they weren't. The room contained a second hand desk, two old, old, grey chairs (one moved, one in the process of being sat on), a wall safe, a fireplace without a fire, a bit of light grey carpet, a coat stand with coat and bonnet, and a visitor. Everything was neat, tidy and functional. I looked around slowly, carefully. I breathed. I walked across the room in a business-like manner and placed myself in my violated chair behind my desk and looked at my visitor.

She was a frail old woman dressed in a long black dress, grey shawl, and tight bun with a lethal looking hair slide. From the back she seemed very peaceful as she stared down into the empty fireplace, in some kind of geriatric trance. She seemed to have made herself completely at home. I reached in my pocket to get a cigarette, looked at the woman and thought better of it. I picked up a pen from my desk and started twirling it in my fingers. I had been having problems remembering things but I had no difficulty remembering this dame. I breathed, 'Aunty Mary.' I said a little too loudly, 'What are you doing here, again?'

'It's about another murder, cariad, I'm ashamed to say.'

'Whoa. Whoa. I'm getting a sense of Deja vu here. What can I help you with Aunty Mary?'

'I need to talk to you, cariad. It's about a murder.'

'Which one?'

'Oh Samael, don't you remember? Young Lily.'

'Oh course I remember, Aunty Mary. It's just that a few days ago you were here telling me about, you know, another murder.'

'Ah yes. Young Cai. A bad business. Poor Cai, Gorffwys mewn hedd.'

I spoke softly and tenderly, 'but Aunty Mary you killed him. You shot him. Remember?'

'That's true. Yes. I did. That's why I wanted to come and see you today.'

'So you killed Lily as well?'

This accusation slash question shocked Aunty Mary, 'of course not, cariad. How could I? What do you think I am? I just wanted to come and tell you that I <u>didn't</u> kill her, you see?'

I had started to lose the will to live, 'Why would I care, Aunty Mary?'

'Because it's your case now isn't it?'

'No. It most definitely is not.'

She leaned over, conspiratorially, 'I think you'll find it is my dear. That's what I pay you for.'

I hadn't realised the shilling was a retainer for all the murders Aunty Mary was going to be involved in. I decided I would need to increase my prices if that was the going rate. 'Really.' I said. I was tired. It had been a late, troubled night and ironically it was now that I found myself drifting off.

'Poor dab.' She said shaking her head. 'I spent a lot of time with her recently. Trying to help. She helped me a lot you know.'

'Lily?'

'She taught me a lot. Even how to shoot a gun.' Aunty Mary continued. Then she stopped suddenly. She started to get up.

'Here Aunty Mary let me help you.'

I helped Aunty Mary put on her ancient grey fur coat and black bonnet then walked her out.

I wandered back to my desk. I put a Lucky Strike in my mouth and stared out of the window. It was grey, but not raining, yet. This is what passed for a beautiful day in Wales. A bit different from Atlanta I thought.

Bobby Jones' Remembers

Nassau Country Club, New York, 8th July 1923

I first met 'Calamity Jane' just before the first practice round of the 1923 US Open at Inwood. It was Sunday 8th July. I had been having something of a torrid time of my golf as I recall. I had been down in the dumps a while and needed something good to happen. Some final piece of the jigsaw if you like. I had played well from tee to green but not going that final furlong. Putting. It was the putting that kept letting me down. Badly. My career had stalled, it's fair to say. Anyway it was the Sunday before the practice rounds began I went to see an old mate of mine, Jimmy Maiden, brother of my great friend Stewart. Jimmy, who I had grown up with in Atlanta, was now professional at the Nassau Country Club, just a spit away from Inwood.

Stewart and I went over to see him. He was waiting for us on the on the putting green. He had the ugliest looking implement I had ever seen in his hands. He was getting holing those putts though. So I had a look at it. I held it in my hands, and I'll love to say the earth moved, but well it didn't. It was as ugly close up as it was from a distance. It looked awful. It was rusty and sort of beat up, and no doubt had several owners before it ever got to me. It was too short and too light. The gopher wood / hickory shaft was cracked and held together with glue and three sections of black linen whipping, giving it the appearance of a snake. It was a goose-necked implement made in Scotland that bore the mark of 'St. Andrew', probably the address of the man who repaired the club's shaft and grip. It seemed that the original had been altered, and added to, many times I suspect. The only original part of the club seemed to be the shaft. This was a strange combination of hickory, which was usual, and gopher wood which definitely was not. I had it examined by experts later, and it was unique. That was all they could agree on.

I tried a few putts and things started to change, within me. It felt real nice. I holed a few short putts. I tried a few longer putts and holed them as well. I just felt like I was never going to miss. I holed twenty four out of the first twenty five putts I had with Jane, no word of a lie, and that was that. I never let her out of my sight after that. She went everywhere with me. Mary joked that I took that club out more often that her. I admitted it. I did. We won that first US Open in 1923 and many, many more after that. She retired when I did after a long and eventful career.

No-one knows who came up with the name. Jimmy said that the person who gave him the putter on that Saturday morning had given it to him with a message to look after her and give it to someone who would use it. He told Jimmy that she had had a long and honourable life already and wanted some glory in her final years. He'd never seen the chap before, or since. Strange, isn't it?

16 Safe

I stopped myself thinking. I had work to do. I put the key I had lifted from Aunty Mary's coat pocket onto the desk. I turned it over in my hand. It was quite big, old and brassy. Not a door key. It was the key to the Golf Club safe. I had seen it for many years in her pocket. Often I had put my hand in Aunty Mary's pocket looking for sweets only to find the key. This had not happened for many years, I should add, at least twenty. The coat hadn't changed, nor the key. I laid it carefully on the desk. I opened my drawer to find there was no gun where a gun would really be if this were Los Angeles instead of Mynydd Eimon. I sighed a little. I picked up my hat from the coat stand, I did actually have a hat (it was a dark grey fedora) and left the office. I retrieved my own key to lock the office door behind me. There are mythological villages in Wales where there is, allegedly, an inbuilt trust and community spirit. We are a giving, trusting and caring people, apparently. I didn't seem to have been blessed with that particular Welsh gene. I locked the door and then rattled the handle twice to make sure it was properly locked.

I walked distractedly north along Alma Road. The houses were all the same – terraced, grey, cramped, old, cold, functional, miner-built, not cute not cute at all. I turned right into Waterloo Road. I passed the 'Square' that was more of an isosceles triangle than any quadrilateral. I saw that there was a light on in the church, thought about going in, didn't, and continued. I turned onto the mountain road, called Mountain Road, toward the golf club. This was the final road of Mynydd Eimon.

Mynydd Eimon was a small, squeezed village where the road stopped because it crashed into the mountain. There was no passing traffic through Mynydd Eimon. It was a dead end village. If you were in Mynydd Eimon you were in it for a reason. The only viable reason was that you lived here. I looked up at the sky. It was, unsurprisingly, grey. I felt trapped. You remember that programme about a man who felt that he was a prisoner in Wales? In Portmeirion it was. The prisoner it was called. Well, that's me.

It was a steep climb to the golf club and as I reached the top of the track I could see the white snow across the black mountains in the distance and a smattering of red and yellow flags positioned along the horizon. It was cold, very cold. The sign on a post at the entrance to the driveway of the golf course said 'Visitors Welcome' – this wasn't true. There were few visitors, they were never welcomed and they never returned. Somehow the club survived on its handful of members and the occasional inbred social function in the Clubhouse.

Yet there never seemed to be any panic about finance. I had been a member since I was eleven years of age yet had never received a request for golf fees. I attributed this to the attitude of the treasurer and the incompetence of the secretary and committee.

The clubhouse was a squat, grim, functional building. The kindest way to describe it was - unremarkable. I approached the, presumably deserted, clubhouse carefully. There was no sign of anyone stirring. I opened the door and went in. The corridor was decorated with expensive wallpaper and a plush burgundy carpet that totally deadened my footsteps. I passed at the trophy cabinet with an array of silver cups and plates inscribed with names of past champions.

On the wall next to the cabinet I saw an empty cabinet. There was the inscription underneath, 'Calamity Jane – presented to Mynydd Eimon Golf Club by Friends of Mynydd Eimon'. Calamity Jane had left the building.

I knocked softly on the door of the secretary's office. I counted to ten waiting for no-one to reply then gently opened the door. The safe was in the corner of the room, behind the writing table. I lit a Lucky

Strike to clear my head and think. Eventually I took the key out of my pocket and opened the very old-fashioned safe. The door of the safe looked old and very solid. It opened easily, smoothly and deathly quietly though.

There was a lot of money in the safe in a range of differing denominations. There were a number of forms, a gun and an old book / folder that looked as if it should have had a sticker on it saying, 'Old folder with lots of interesting information in it'. It was black, ancient and had three large, thick, old-fashioned elastic bands around it holding loose papers and photographs. The cover had a label that said 'ACCOUNTS BOOK' – which it clearly wasn't. I took off the elastic bands and flicked quickly through the book at diary entries, old photographs, newspaper cuttings, pieces of ancient parchment, Latin verses and what looked like recipes. I re-tied the elastic bands around the folder and put it under my coat. It was thick and heavy.

I walked back along the corridor to the front door. I looked around. There was no-one around. It was quiet, too quiet, as they say. I walked back down the hill toward the village thinking hard. I was mainly thinking about the putter. Where had it gone? I was also thinking how phenomenally easy it had been to get the key and take the folder from the safe. The clubhouse had not been locked, no-one had been in the club, or on the course, or on Mountain Road, or anywhere I had been. Unusual. It was almost as if....

Yeah I know. Oh, and whose gun was that in the safe? Not Aunty Mary's. She always kept hers close.

17 Partners

I went into my office with the folder under my arm. The door was unlocked. I should have been surprised and worried. I wasn't. I looked around the waiting room. No-one there and nothing disturbed. I carefully clutched the handle of the inner door. I opened the door gently to see my sister seated near the fireplace reading Vanity Fair. I tried to put the folder in the safe without my sister noticing. She looked up at me, smiled a little and mouthed, 'Oh please' in a patronising fashion. I put the folder on the table. She seemed in a happier mood today.

'How did you get in, sis?' I asked, casually.

She shrugged it aside, 'I've something to tell you. Something I remembered.'

I opened my desk drawer and brought out a bottle of whiskey. 'Drink?' I asked

She looked up, 'you know I do.' she replied.

She lit a Chesterfield and offered one to me. I accepted.

I poured a drink for both of us in the paper cups I kept in my bottom drawer, for just such an occasion. I handed one to my sister, 'here's looking at you kid.'

'Cheers bro. So what's in the book?' she was referring to the folder I had surreptitiously placed on the table.

'I don't know yet. I'll tell you when I find out.'

'Seems like you don't trust me bruv? That's not good for partners is it?'

'Who says we're partners?'

'I thought we agreed? Ah well. Let's pretend we have.'

She stood up and move around to the table. She touched the folder, inquisitively then changed tack. 'So, detective,' she said, raising her cup, 'who killed Lily?' She finished off her drink and poured herself another. 'What are your thoughts partner? Talk me through your deductive reasoning? What's the motive?' She asked all these questions before I could respond to the first one.

'You want me to talk about 'means, motive and opportunity',' I said.

'OK. If that's how you solve your crimes. What's the motive then? Lily seemed dumb enough to be safe from everyone.'

Seren circled around the room constantly, confusingly, like a tall, elegant vulture.

'Who knows? You tell me sis. Why would anyone want to kill Lily?'

'Exactly. You're the detective - you work it out.' She was now standing near the coat stand.

'Come on Sis. You're my partner now. You tell me. You know people around here better than I do. What could anyone gain by killing Lily?'

Seren thought carefully, from behind my desk. She conscientiously put out her cigarette in the ashtray. I did the same. There was a moment's silence. Then she continued, 'Well perhaps it had something to do with Cai's death. You know it's a bit of a coincidence.' She said as she sat in my chair.

'Possibly,' I said.

'Revenge maybe.' She stood up.

It was hypnotic watching her move. I pretended to thinking carefully, as if the thought was just occurring to me, 'Who? How about you sis? You had a thing with Cai didn't you?'

'Fuck you bro.' She was more pretend upset than upset but I thought I had touched a nerve, especially when she said, 'I knew a lot about Lily.' from near the door.

She had always changed the subject like this when she was little. Just when you opened a little gap in her defences she managed to redirect you. Perhaps this constant walking around was part of her psychology. It's always harder to hit a moving target, and all that. Or maybe I'm just over-thinking it.

'Oh,' I said, then followed up with, 'Sis, Sit down please. You are doing my head in.'

She did, for a short while, and said, 'Yes. She could be a manipulative cow. I reckon she killed Cai.'

'Stop it sis. We all know Aunty Mary killed Cai.'

'Yes, but why? Aunty Mary isn't clever or spiteful enough to do it on her own back. Someone was playing her. Don't you think?' She was up and moving toward the door now.

I did think that. But why Lily? What secrets did she have?

'Think about it bro,' she said from over her shoulder as she left with a great dramatic swoosh.

18 Photographs

Alone in my office I took the elastic bands from the folder. It was a mess. I opened the 'Accounts Book' and fairly carefully put all the assorted documents on the table. It was interesting. There were tickets, invoices, receipts. There were photographs, documents, a little book, newspaper cuttings and more and more. I placed them on the desk and cleared a space to examine what looked like the prime deposition - a large, old accounting book. It was russet and venerable. It was lovely to touch with the cover a sort of leathery, goat skin cover with Etruscan binding. It felt smooth, used and ancient. It turned to the beginning of the book. There were columns separates by double red lines, with headings at the top of each column - DATE, INITIALS, CR, DR, BALANCE. All completed in Aunty Mary's scrawling, sprawling words and numbers. I read the title on each double page. I grabbed a pen and some paper from my drawer and started to make, what I felt, was a pertinent list. This seemed to be the essence of the book. I made a list of locations and dates. I ignored the detailed invoices and records and other distracting bits of information. It took me a while to untangle it all but I eventually arrived at;

Transvaal 1895;

Shengting Province 1899;

Chihuahua 1910;

Sarejavo 1914;

Petrograde 1917;

Dublin 1922;

New York 1923;

Philadelphia 1924;

Columbus Ohio 1926;

Liverpool 1930;

Philadelphia 1930;

Wanpaoshan 1931;

Lausanne 1932;

Berlin 1933.

When I lit a cigarette and perused the entire list, some of the dates hurt. Not only the Boxer Rebellion, the assassination of 1914 or the Dublin trips. These were obviously truly horrific events and it shocked me to see them. But I am, as you know, quite selfish and I remember Hoylake, Liverpool in 1930. I remember sitting in the clubhouse on the final day watching the crowd and waiting nervously for Leo to finish to see if I was Open champion. I wonder if he had been in the crowd, watching and waiting with me. As I say I am incredibly egoistical. I looked at the list and tried to reconcile it with my memories of before I left Mynydd Eimon. I remember him leaving for long periods. He said it was part of his job. I remember him telling us when we were little that he was a conflict resolution consultant. I understood that now. It's quite funny in a not-very-appropriate way. At the time it could have been anything. I wondered about Berlin and whether he were still there now. Today.

I pushed the list and the accounts book to one side and picked up a number of photos. There were photos of Bobby Jones' holding his battered old goose-necked putter, a picture of Bobby Jones on his wedding day with 'childhood sweetheart Mary Rice Malone'. There were photos of Bobby Jones in a variety of golfing poses. There was a photograph of two children playing with a sculpture of Bobby Jones. On the back was written 'Clara and Bobby'. There were photos of Bobby Jones at Augusta, Bobby Jones at Merion, Bobby Jones at St Andrews, Bobby Jones at Hoylake.

There were other photos, a photo of a muddy Bobby Jones after a golf tournament, a photo of Clara, Bobby junior and Mary Ellen (a wife I can barely remember). I looked at the Wedding day photographs that could have been of anyone. There was an ancient looking manila envelope addressed to me. I thought I'd save this little gem for later. I found bible texts, old poems (or were the spells).

I found a small book with the title 'The Story of Golf'. Inside were a dozen or so hand written, parchment pages. I read the first page;

It had been a hard ten years but now it was nearly over. The clouds were dark and the sea looked angry. They had been a month in Patras and their journey was coming to an end.

They walked further along the seafront towards the rocks. Andrew bent over to pick up a longish piece of driftwood and started examining it. 'Gopher Wood' he announced.

'Wasn't that the wood from the ark?' I asked.

'It was,' announced Andrew as he started swinging it. We found some circular pebbles and before long were hitting the pebbles along the deserted beach. The sun had appeared through the clouds and it seemed like this was the final perfect moment.

Suddenly the moment of peace and tranquillity was ruined as the wind sprung up and the waves crashed against the rocks they were walking on. Aegeas and twenty one men soldiers rushed forward and grabbed Andrew. They began dragging him away toward a decussate cross. He leaned over to me and resigned to his fate, whispered, 'Remember these last moments, Maximila'

I put the book with the accounts book. I explored more. I did recognise Aunty Mary's writing on the invoices and accounts pinned to various train, ship and air tickets. There were invoices for guns, bullets and meals. There were a number of clippings of golfer Bobby Jones clipped together chronologically from July 1923 to July 1930, each delicately clipped clipping was from a range of newspapers from either America or Britain, Some regional, some national;

'CROWDS HAIL JONES ON RETURN TO U.S. 'from the Memphis Evening Appeal;

'BOBBY JONES WINS IN OPEN' from the Daily Express;

'JONES WINS BIG GOLF TITLE FOR FOURTH IN ROW' from the Bethlehem Globe-Times;

'GRAND SLAM JONES.' from somewhere else.

There was a quote from Bernard Darwin, greatest golf writer, and grandson of Charles Darwin, writing about Bobby, 'The price he pays for his success is too much'.

I read a page cut out of a golf magazine;

He was only twenty-eight years old and Bobby Jones announced his retirement from all golfing competition. The greatest golfer the world had ever known had played in his last championship. He had finished off the seven fat years with thirteen major championships. In the closing year 1930, he had accomplished the impossible - winning all four major titles.

I recalled an incident in an upstairs room at the Interlachen Club a few months earlier. I put my hand on his shoulder and asked him: 'Bobby, when are you going to quit this darned game?'

Bobby looked a shade more serious. 'I don't know," he said, 'but pretty soon, I think. I am awfully tired.'

I read these with interest and a churning in my insides. It was like being hit in the stomach. Not hard, but constantly. Blow after blow after blow. Like an aching tooth though I kept touching it. I kept returning to the children's photographs. One in particular of Clara and Bobby junior, playing with a sculpture of Bobby Jones. I remember that day. It was the summer of 1927 and I'd just won the Open for the second time. This time at St Andrews. More than that the Scottish crowd now loved me. I went home to see my children and thought nothing could ever surpass this - the pinnacle of my career, my wife, my home, my children. Nothing.

I looked and looked at the photo, remembering, hurting. I lit a cigarette and burnt the photograph slowly over the ashtray. It was gone. Whatever life I had was gone. I was on my own.

19 Unexpected Visitors

I had my back to the door when they walked in. I had gathered up all the documented and put them in the safe. I had just locking the safe when I heard a noise, turned around and saw a rare sight. At first I didn't recognise what it was. Something flashed through my mind instantly.

I remember reading the story of Christopher Columbus. The story was about his first voyage to the Caribbean islands. As Columbus' ships, the Santa Maria, Nina, and Pinta, approached the islands on October 11 1492, I even remembered the date, the natives could not see them. One account describes how the shaman of the islanders noticed that the waves washing up on the shore produced an unusual pattern. From this observation the shaman realised that something unusual was happening and looked harder out to sea. Eventually his mind focused and he saw the ships at a fairly close range. He then had to persuade the people to also see the ships. The explanation for this was that as the natives had no concept of large ships and they simply could not see them.

I tried hard and I could see two shapes. After a few seconds I began to identify these shapes. They were dressed strangely. They were both wearing dark, coarse navy blue serge uniforms, shiny buttons with leather accoutrements. I had read about them, seen photographs in children's book when I was in the infant school. One of the shaped had a spiked helmet, whilst the other, the more senior by the look of it, had a matching cap.

I looked at the dark, coarse outfits again and finally it all clicked. They were policemen.

'Mr Watcher?' The taller one asked as he shook my hand.

'Yes.' I replied.

'Detective Inspector Eurion.' He carried on shaking my hand. 'And this,' indicating his colleague, 'is Sergeant Rhydion'. I shook Sergeant Rhydion's hand. They both kept their gloves on. 'Shiny buttons and leather gloves', I thought, for no particular reason. Sergeant Rhydion had taken off his helmet and was holding it tightly under his arm. I indicated that they should sit down. In a strange, ridiculously formal manner Sergeant Rhydion looked at his boss and waited for him to sit. Then he moved his chair six inches behind Detective Inspector Eurion's chair a little - expressing his subservience perfectly. Sergeant Rhydion looked a little uncomfortable with his spiked helmet under his arm. It was almost as if he had never had to manage this cumbersome piece of equipment before. He held it. Then moved it to his other arm. Then put it on the floor. Then picked it up. Then tried to get his brand new pen and brand new notepad from his pocket. Then he put the helmet on the table. It was uncomfortable to watch. As I say, it was almost as if he had never had to manage this cumbersome piece of equipment before. Detective Inspector gave a knowing stare at Sergeant Rhydion and the Sergeant put it on the floor next to him.

I was fascinated by them. It was all I could do to not touch their uniforms. I was staring at Sergeant Rhydion's spiked helmet on my table when Detective Inspector Eurion spoke. I didn't hear him initially as my mind was whirling. I had seen a number of American policemen in films. 'You'll never take me alive coppers', I managed to stop myself from saying. It was captivating. Absolutely captivating.

I realised that detective Inspector Eurion had been talking to me for a while. I tuned in to what he was saying. I heard the word 'Cardiff.' I must have looked puzzled as he stopped and repeated himself. 'Mr Watcher, I was just saying that myself and Sergeant Rhydion are from Cardiff.'

'Well done' I said.

I noticed Rhydion was writing this down in his pristine notebook. It was painful to watch him writing with his gloves on.

Detective Inspector Eurion continued, 'We are investigating the death of....' he consulted his brand new notebook, as all real policemen would do at this point. Eurion had a strange accent. Not from Cardiff, I don't think, although to be fair the number of accents I could identify outside America was slim. He had an accent I wasn't familiar with at all. It sounded foreign. But understandable. No, not foreign, almost robotic. Added to this he had long black hair, almost womanly, sweeping down his face onto his dark collar. It would have looked strange but for the fact that Sergeant Rhydion also had long hair, blonde. It was over his shoulders almost obscuring the numbers on his stiff buttoned up collar. Maybe be the style in Cardiff I thought.

'....Lily Llewellyn.' He looked up from his notebook, 'I understand you found Mrs. Llewellyn.'

I related my story. He nodded. Rhydion made notes. I lit a cigarette and offered one to each of them.

'No thanks. Not when we're on duty.' Eurion answered for both.

They listened politely. I had the feeling they knew all this anyway.

'How do you know all this anyway?' I asked.

'We don't obviously' Eurion replied, 'No one has told us this before.'

'Who called to tell you Lily was dead, 'I asked.

Detective Inspector Eurion looked at Sergeant Rhydion. No help there. 'I think we'll be asking the questions mister watcher, if you don't mind?'

I didn't. I was fascinated by the sheer amateurism of the performance.

'Have you any idea who would want to harm Mrs. Llewellyn.' asked Eurion.

I didn't. Eurion closed his notebook.

I stood up, expecting Eurion to stand up and say 'Very well sir. Thank you for that. We'll be in touch if we need anything further from you.'

He didn't. Rhydion grabbed my arms from behind and Eurion punched me in the stomach.

'Don't mess us around Mr Watcher. Tell us why Lily was murdered. Tell us, you hear. What was she hiding for you? What was she hiding?' said Rhydion.

I moaned. I was perfectly happy to tell them everything I knew. They weren't that keen to listen. It seemed they were, ironically, making a statement themselves. I was on the floor and they were oofing and groofing and grunting a lot, without actually kicking me. They didn't seem that keen on hurting me. They were the ones doing most of the sound effects. They were extremely careful with my hands, ribs, face. It was the gentlest, but loudest beating I'd ever had. Well, I hadn't had too many.

Eurion suddenly said, 'Very well sir. Thank you for that. We'll be in touch if we need anything further from you.'

And they left. I stayed on the floor for a moment or two. I reached in my pocket and got out a cigarette. I lit it. I reached up to the desk and grabbed a glass and a bottle. I poured a drink. I smoked and drank. I know it was early but this was an unusual day. I'd seen my first policeman, and I'd had a pretend beating. Life was getting stranger. Then I had a phone call to say that my presence was requested at the golf club.

20 New Client

I wandered back up Mountain Road to the golf club. The only remarkable feature of my journey was that it wasn't raining. A rare turn of events indeed. I could see that the club was now inhabited. There were lights on and everything. I went in, walked along the plush carpeted corridor to the secretary's office. I knocked.

'Come in'.

I went in.

Uncle Daniel stood up, 'Samael how are you today, dear boy?'

'Been better,' I replied, 'I've just been visited by the police.'

He laughed. 'Oh Samael, Samael, Samael. Whatever did they want?' He smiled and looked at me. I didn't believe this was the biggest surprise he had ever had in his life.

'Just a little chat.' I replied.

'About whom?'

I looked at him. 'About the death of your wife.'

I looked closely at him as I said this and then started singing in my head, 'No alarms and no surprises'.

Silence for a minute. He poured himself a drink, poured one for me and sat back in his chair. He indicated the other chair across the desk. I sat.

'Sam,' he said a little seriously, 'I want you to find out who killed Lily.'

'Your wife.'

'My dead wife.' He said pointedly.

'Who knew you were married?' I asked.

He ignored me, 'I liked Lily. I loved Lily.' It was difficult to tell how upset he was. He was such a good actor. He was really good at the happy, jolly, fat man role. Come to think of it I had rarely, if ever, seen him play any other part.

He finished his drink and gave me a shilling, 'I think that's the going rate isn't it?' He smiled.

'Why was Cai killed,' I asked.

'It's obvious isn't it? One in, one out. You won and he came second. You know that?'

'How do I know that?'

'Aunty Mary told you. You killed Cai by winning.'

I finished my drink in silence. I knew all this. I was more concerned with how many people knew about Uncle Daniel and Lily. It was hardly a secret. I'd seen them trying not to look at each other at the funeral. It's even more of a giveaway than kissing I public I think. It explained why she had volunteered to work for me free. Daniel could keep an eye on me presumably for my father. And perhaps Lily's manipulation of Aunty Mary was because someone else was pulling her strings. Who better than a husband?

I stood up with another headache. I left Daniel drinking and staring into space. I walked back along the plush corridor and out of the door. I bumped into Michael.

21 Golf with Michael

'Why did you send Stan and Ollie ahead of you?' I asked Michael.

'Pardon?'

'You know, Dumb and Dumber, Rhydion and Eurion.'

'Oh I don't know. I thought it might cheer you up.'

'And let me know Lily was married to Daniel.'

'Yes there was that', he paused, 'but you knew that already right?'

I said nothing.

'I wanted to introduce some new characters. We need to balance up the village. There are too many bad guys here.'

He seemed to be serious. I asked, 'And you are the good guys?'

'We are.'

'Which makes us the bad guys.'

'Us?' smiled Michael.

'Well, Uncle Daniel and his entourage.'

He decided to make a point. 'Your father and his legion.'

'One man's legion is another man's host.' I remarked.

He smiled. 'I didn't think you were taking sides, Samael?'

'Neither did I.' I replied, and meant it.

We looked at each other not warily or suspiciously as such, more intriguingly. Like chess players, or boxers waiting for the first move. Well, chess players really. There was no hint of violence. It was incredibly civilised.

'Come on Sam, fancy a knock?' he asked, cheerily.

I did. We wandered to the changing rooms, chatting quite amicably about this and that. He had a lovely manner, a lovely way of making you feel important, calm and listened to. He had that charm, that charisma, carisma.

Michael went to his locker to get his golf clubs. I changed my shoes, grabbed my clubs and wandered out towards the first tee. I had never met Michael before, in the flesh, so to speak but he had played a large part in my growing up. He was always there as a thing, an image, an icon. Always there, always there, always on my shoulder, so to speak. Oh, Michael is an angel, if you hadn't guessed. He's famous. You may have heard of him. Archangel? As angel hierarchies go, he's kind of the top angel. I recognised him from the drawings I used to see in the book of bible stories we had in the church. Blonde, old-fashioned. Like a youngish version of Alan Ladd, which seems a slightly unusual simile I guess, but there you are. Is it a simile when you compare someone to another person? Eternally youthful would be a good way to describe Michael, and Alan Ladd, I guess. He definitely looks like one of the good guys. You couldn't imagine him descending from the heavens and smiting and fornicating like some of the other angels, can you? He did remind me of Cai though, now that I'd seen him close up. The same mouth really. But, surely, surely Michael would not have 'saw and lusted' after the 'beautiful and comely daughters'? Would he?

'No Sam, I wouldn't'. Michael interrupted my thoughts as he walked up behind me. 'I told you I'm one of the good guys.'

I realized I had been speaking aloud. Something I notice I've started to do recently.

'Sorry', I mouthed.

'I hear you're quite a golfer now?' he remarked as we ambled out to the first tee.

'Apparently so.' I replied tersely.

'Sorry Sam. I shouldn't tease you.' He leaned his golf bag against the bench next to the first tee and took his driver out, a bit tentatively.

'How long is it since you've played?' I asked politely.

'Many, many moons,' he answered and examined his club lovingly as you would examine a thing you cared about and had many good memories with. I had few of those objects. My clubs were from my other life. My childhood. I didn't particularly want to treasure those memories.

He smiled. 'OK Sam. Your honour.'

I starting swinging my driver loosening up. I was warmed up from this morning, but that was different. This was a competition. I had always been quite competitive. In most things. I took a deep breath and stepped forward to address the ball.

'How is your father Sam?' Michael asked casually.

I stepped back.

'Sorry', he said.

I stopped and answered him honestly. 'I don't know. I haven't seen him. I'm not involved.' I said. I looked him in the eye. 'Really. I'm not involved. I'm neutral, just like Spain.'

Michael looked surprised.

'In the war. Spain was neutral.'

He smiled, 'Sorry Sam. I'm just amused how viciously you defend your neutrality.'

I started again.

I was surprisingly nervous as I teed off with the archangel looking intently at my swing. Luckily I got a good shot off - long and straight.

'Good ball.' he remarked.

Then Michael hit a decent shot, not quite as long, but straight. Arrow straight. We wandered down the fairway together.

I realized that I didn't know what to call him? Saint Michael? Archangel Michael? He who is like God?

90

'Just Michael would be fine,' he smiled. I was doing it again. I really should stop thinking aloud. I'd make a terrible poker player.

'Michael,' I tried the name out. It felt OK, 'I've always wanted to ask you something. How much can you tell me about my father and your ... disagreement?'

'Let's not talk shop, eh Sam. I thought we would just have a nice game of golf.

'Sorry.'

'I'm teasing Sam. You can ask me anything.'

'Look. We were close once and then we, well we saw things differently. But it's only work Sam. It's not everything. We rarely see each other these days.'

'Join the club.'

'We move in different circles, you know. He has his life. I have mine.'

'Different bosses?'

He addressed his ball in the middle of the fairway and smiled, 'No. The same boss really.' He stopped and thought, 'Well I assume so.' He hit a lovely shot into the heart of the green.

I hit my shot onto the green as well and we carried on, as if we were out on a Sunday stroll. We chatted a little about golf, the weather, the state of the greens and other trivialities as we finished the first hole. We both two-putted for par. We walked to the next tee and I asked, 'Do you mind if I ask you something else?'

'Sure. Anything Sam.'

'It's a bit silly really but no-one will tell me. I asked any number of people in the village but no-one would tell me.'

'OK.'

'It's about angels.'

'OK.'

91

'Where are the wings?'

He looked at me as if I were a child.

'Don't believe everything you read in the bible.' He smiled, 'Not that it says anything at all about angels having wings. It's a pagan thing anyway.' He explained. 'It's a PR thing. Angels are just angels - good, bad, happy, sad, low handicappers, scratch golfers.'

'Pretend policemen' I chided.

He smiled.

We played on. It was close. Michael was a good golfer. Solid. Unfussy. We reached the turn with me leading by a shot. We stopped for a rest and a cigarette.

Michael suddenly went all serious on me, 'Look Sam. I know what happened with your trip to America and I wasn't happy about it.'

I shrugged.

'But what could I do? He is your father after all.'

'Why did you and my father really fall out?' I asked.

'You know it's in the bible.'

'I don't believe everything they say in the bible. Anyway, this was before all that though, wasn't it?'

'Sort of. Yes. We had a disagreement'

'Over my mother?'

'Sort of. Anyway it's all over now. Your shot.'

And that was all. That was all I got from him.

We finished the round. It was a close game. He was polite. He conceded a number of putts that I don't think I would have let him have. He was just a nice angel. I beat him as well, which I was surprising delighted with, although I hid it well.

'Well played Sam. You're quite a player.'

'Thank you Michael.'

We walked off the final green to the changing rooms.

'I guess you'll be investigating Lily's murder?' he asked.

'Maybe. I don't like to talk about my work. But if I were is there any help you can give me?'

'Me? No. First I'd heard about it was this morning when I arrived.'

'Oh and where had you been?'

He looked at me.

'Sam. Surely you're not going to ask an archangel their whereabouts on the night of the murder?'

He looked again

'You are.' He said. Then continued, 'Oh Sam I can't tell you that. You're the enemy. Sorry. You're neutral I know. But, I've been working. All a bit hush hush at the moment.'

We shook hands and changed our shoes and put the clubs away. We said our goodbyes and Michael went into the clubhouse.

I walked down the hill wondering what work could be hush hush for an archangel. Practically anything I concluded. I then realized that for all his geniality and seeming openness I didn't trust the archangel Michael as far as I could putt him. This sounded like quite an odd sentence. But it was true. He was lying to me. I knew it and he knew that I knew it.

22 Walking Down That Hill

I walked slowly down the hill back to the village. I had one case to solve. The murder of one Lily Llewellyn. I thought I'd better find out a little bit about her. I suspected that she was connected to Llewellyn. I knew now that she was connected through marriage as it happens. The question now was, or one of them at least, where was the child? Or children? These weren't the days where people married for love. Especially not lusty angels. I had suspected that he paid her to work for me. That was confirmed. Now, I had to find a new secretary. I didn't think Uncle Daniel would be keen to cough up the money for another one, now that I knows that he knows I know. I lit a Lucky Strike. I thought. I lit another cigarette and thought again and again. Harder, this time.

What did I really know? Exactly. Pretty much nothing. I knew Aunty Mary had killed Cai. I didn't know who pushed her buttons though. I knew Lily was dead. I didn't know who was responsible. However Michael's sudden arrival must indicate something. He seemed to be worried about something and wanted to plant some knowledge on me for some reason. What did this have to do with my return? Was there anyone here that would tell me the truth or at least some approximation of the truth? Perhaps I needed a priest. As it happens I was in luck. I could see the church a few yards from me. The door was open. I spotted a praying mantis dressed in black in the doorway. Almost as if he were waiting for me. The priest. My priest. Our father. Father Barry. He smiled at me.

23 Don't Lift Your Petticoat

As I approached the church Father Barry disappeared inside. I walked through the great door archway and entered slowly, warily. Father Barry had somehow got to the far end of the church. He was standing leaning on a bench. I looked around. The church was god knows how many centuries old. Father Barry was God knows how many centuries old. I was starting to feel old.

I looked again as my eyes adjusted to the grey holy light and saw that he wasn't alone. Where I had thought he was leaning on the edge of a pew he was in fact walking hand in hand with Aunty Mary. They walked towards the aisle slowly, horribly slowly. They looked like misery and his nanna about to be betrothed. Bela Lugosi and Miss Haversham. The air of gloom and despondency was almost palpable. I watched in a kind of possessed, spellbound trance.

I watched entranced for a long, long time before I approached them. They had now, finally, sat together on the front row in a pew. I sat alongside them, next to Father Barry, with Aunty Mary on his right. I stared at the altar.

Aunty Mary moved her head forward and stared straight at me around Father Barry, 'Don't blame me, cariad. I was only doing what I was told.' She announced.

I did blame her. She shot him. He was my only friend in the world. Granted I didn't like him that much, but he was my only friend. I suddenly felt incredibly angry. 'So why the fuck did you do it?' I asked.

She shrugged.

'Are you sure you didn't kill Lily as well?' I asked, a little bitchily.

She looked horrified, 'Of course not, Samael. I would never do anything like that.'

I looked at her with a sarcastic 'unbelievable' in my eyes.

'Well who did then?' I asked.

'I'm not really sure, cariad' she replied

'I'm not really sure, cariad?' I retorted quite sarcastically, and childishly really.

Father Barry decided to stage an intervention. 'Now come we can argue all day about who did what and who killed whom and the rights and wrongs but it's not going to bring either of them back is it?' He said. Then followed it up with, 'Paid â chodi pais ar ôl piso'. Don't lift your petticoat after pissing.'

Father Barry didn't look as if he were joking. Merely stating a fact. The time I'd spent back in the village was becoming more and more ridiculous. I was beginning to feel like Marilyn Munster out of The Munsters. The ridiculousness of the situation had thrown me off kilter though and I had calmed down. I breathed deeply, 'Aunty Mary it's generally not a good idea to kill people?' I said.

'I didn't kill her.' She insisted. Then added, looking straight at me, 'but I think it had something to do with you? I heard them arguing about you'.

'Mary'. Father Barry tried to intervene.

'Barry. He's one of us. He needs to know how we resolve misunderstandings.'

They looked at each other as if they were deciding. I pleaded, 'Tell me Aunty Mary. I need to know.'

Aunty Mary told me, 'Daniel and Lily were talking about you. Arguing. 'Should we tell him?' I heard. 'He has a right to know and I'm going to tell him' Lily said. Then Llewellyn said, 'If you do I'll kill you'. They were married you know?'

Father Barry went white. He tried to get between Aunty Mary and me, literally 'Mary. Stop it,' he said, 'You don't know what you're saying.'

I paused. Then said, 'Really? It sounds a bit stage managed doesn't it? 'He has a right to know?' 'If you do I'll kill you.' Come on Aunty Mary. Really?'

'Don't keep asking questions, cariad. Gormod o bwdin dagith gi. Too much pudding will choke a dog.'

Aunty Mary was getting quite agitated, 'I'm only doing what I'm told. I'm only doing what I'm told. I'm only doing what I'm told.' She stood up and walked back down the aisle, still mumbling to herself. I walked down the aisle beside her and placed the key back in her coat pocket.

I looked at Father Barry. He shrugged, 'Sam. Look. Just leave things be, yes? Let sleeping dogs lie. Just accept things as they are.'

'We all know that's not going to happen don't we?' I said and left.

24 Back at the Ranch

I returned to my office. I opened the door, walked in and saw nothing. No moved chairs, no receptionist. Nothing had been disturbed following my cartoon assault a few hours ago. I opened the safe, took out the folder and lay it on the desk whilst I poured myself a large drink.

I drank it in one gulp. I must have been thirsty, or something. I poured myself another. Then I looked at the remaining contents of the folder in more detail. I flipped through the photographs, the receipts, bible verses, press cuttings and came to the thing I had been avoiding. It was an old manila envelope addressed to me. I looked at the back and there was that contraption with a piece of string threaded between two circular paper buttons to keep the envelope fastened. I had put it aside when I first saw it. I didn't like the look of it. I was pretty sure it wasn't going to be good news. The writing on the envelope was not in Aunty Mary's ornate hand, but Lily's tight, functional hand. I unwound the string carefully and reached inside for the sheet of paper. This was not in Lily's hand either, but scrawled in barely legible red ink by an unknown hand. Or something that looked like red ink. It was a list of names;

Samyaza Watcher
Daniel Llewellyn
Amos Caddoc
Pedwar Penn
Barry Abloec
Mary Lileth-Llad
~~Cai Tywysog~~   Samael Watcher

I tried to work out if this was good or bad news. I sat and thought. Thought and smoked. Smoked and drank. For maybe an hour. I still couldn't work it out. I folded it and put it in my pocket. Then I picked up my hat and went out.

25 I am the Rose of Sharon, the Lily of the Valleys

I left my office and walked along Balaclava Road. I turned right onto Inkerman Street, then Lucknow Lane where I suddenly met my sister. She seemed a little lost, and a little vague about where she was coming from or going too. I felt like Jim Carey in a scene from Truman's World. Why was Seren in that place, at that time? It was almost as if she knew....no. That's ridiculous. Or paranoid. Or accurate. She asked where I was going. I told her and she decided she should tag along, being as we were partners and all now. We walked along Lucknow Lane to Waterloo Road and arrived at the rather large garden outside the rather large house of Doctor Amos Caddoc, loose acquaintance of mine, doctor and listee.

We entered the house slash surgery. The waiting room was empty. Rose, Caddoc's receptionist, told us that Dr Caddoc wouldn't be able to see us as he had a busy schedule. I looked around the deserted room.

'Really?' I said, cuttingly.

'He's doing things.' She gave me a 'you wouldn't understand' look and pretended to concentrate hard on her work.

'Let's go Sam.' said Seren.

I had no intention of going anywhere. Rose seemed to recognise me once Lily had uttered my name. Which was strange as we had known each other a while, I thought. Well, some nodding acquaintance at least.

'Ah Sam. You'll be looking for a new secretary.' said Rose.

'Well yes, actually I am.'

Seren lost it a little and began issuing a number of barked orders 'Sam you mercenary bastard.', 'Oy Rose! Press that buzzer. Tell Amos we're coming in.'

When Rose didn't respond quickly enough Seren lost the infinitesimal amount of patience she had left, leaned over the desk and pressed the buzzer herself.

Both Rose and I pretended nothing had happened. 'I'll see you tomorrow Rose, for an interview at nine.' I said.

'That won't be necessary.' Rose replied, 'I'll start at eight thirty.'

'That works as well.' I answered.

The buzzer from inside the doctor's office rang and Amos' voice called out, 'ready now.'

I decided I'd like to keep Amos waiting now, 'So, Rose,' I asked, 'Why weren't at the reception after the funeral?'

'Sam, leave it.' Said Seren.

I looked at my sister. It wasn't like her to be protective of another human being outside the family. 'Just curious sis.' I looked again at Rose, 'Did you know Lily at all?'

'Ready now'. Amos' voice.

'Sam,' warned Seren, 'you're out of your depth.'

Seren looked at me, then at Rose. Rose seemed unmoved. This was the receptionist I wanted.

'Ready to see you now.' Came Amos' voice.

'Let's just go and see Amos, shall we bro?' said Seren.

I stood up.

'You may go in now,' said Rose. Then added, 'He's in the room marked Dr Caddoc.' Which I felt was a little unnecessary.

Seren stood as well.

Rose leaned over the desk and touched Seren's arm.

'Not you dear,' Rose said to Seren, 'you can stay here with me.'

I walked along the corridor with pictures of lungs, cigarettes, babies and teeth. I knocked and waited for the word. It came immediately.

101

'Come'.

26 The Doctor Is In

The doctor's consulting room was not white. It was a pale blue. There were a number of instruments and implements looking a little disused in a corner. Amos seemed to have little to do with these. Instead he was sitting behind a desk very similar to mine but a little larger. On the desk was his buzzer, a phone, an ash tray and a packet of cigarettes. He got up and moved around the desk to greet me enthusiastically. 'Sam. How are things with you?'

'Oh you know. Interesting' I replied.

He giggled. 'I bet they are, Sam. I bet they are. Sit. Sit.'

I sat sat.

He saw me looking at his pack of Chesterfield cigarettes on the desk. He picked them up and offered one to me. I accepted. He took one himself and lit us both. We both sat back and took a long, long drag.

'What can I do for you Sam?'

'Have a guess Amos?'

He smiled and laughed a little. He was irritatingly jolly.

'I suppose this is about Rose' sister.'

'You could say that, yes. I'm interested in who killed her. I've a client who's asking as well as a couple of pantomime policemen who seem to think I had something to do with it.' I tried to sound worried in the hope it would help.

It didn't. 'Police? Really? In Mynydd Eimon? That can't be right, can it?'

'Well I doubt there are real police.'

'Ah. Yes. Did they have long hair and they never took their gloves off?'

I nodded.

'Sounds like Michael's companions. They're a bit of a joke really. Only naive humans would take them seriously.'

'I did.' I lied.

'Yes, well.' He laughed again, 'Pulling your leg. Joke. They're very convincing, really'

I took a long drag on my Chesterfield. 'So, you seem to know everything Amos. Tell me about Lily?'

'What do you want to know?'

'Anything. I hardly know her. She's worked for me for a couple of days. She just turned up really.'

'Yes. They do that.' I guess he was referring to Rose.

'But why?'

'To look after you, of course. You're like I was, a little Bambi on ice. You need a, oh you know a whatjamarabbit?'

'Thumper.'

'That's it. She's your Thumper. To help you to skate. To learn the ropes.'

'What fucking ropes?' I was started to get a little pretending annoyed. I was desperate to crack the surface of one of these hellish angels.

'Easy tiger,' said Amos, 'It's just one of those things that are organised for you. It was the same with me. We're all on your side. Just relax.'

'But I don't want you to be on my side. I just want you all to leave me alone.' I wasn't sure now if I was pretend angry or really angry.

'Hey. Let it go, Sam. Just leave it.'

I was silent.

'You know Lily was married to Daniel.'

'Yes. Yes. Everyone keeps telling me'

'It's a clue.' He continued playfully.

'No. No. No. Amos. I'm not playing this one. Let's see how this one pans out shall we?' I then presented the argument to him as simple as I could, 'So you are telling me Lily was married to Daniel. Correct?'

Amos nodded.

'I go to someone with this information and they tell me, mmm let me think, oh I don't know, something about someone else. Yes?'

Another nod. 'Yes, like a trade. If you tell, say Seren at the ruins that you know about Lily and Daniel.'

I interrupted 'Then I go to someone else with this info and they tell me something else about someone. I go to them and eventually end up finding Lily's killer. Well I guess there are a few more iterations, red herrings and dead ends. But is that it?'

Amos was thrilled. 'That's it. And I've given you your first clue.'

'But, that's not how this works.' I was exasperated, and not pretending now.

'Of course it is, silly. The girl goes to Spade. Spade goes to Cairo. Cairo goes back to the girl. The girl goes to Gutman. Spade goes to Gutman. Gutman scarpers. Marlow goes to the police and turns the girl in. It's exactly how it works.'

I sighed deeply. 'But it's not like that. Life isn't a computer game, 'The Quest for Lily's killer' where the hero has to solve a number of clues and challenges.' Even as I was saying it. I could hear Amos' next line. I was wrong.

'What's a computer game?'

I tried to explain that I had been playing computer games for years somehow. It was one of the few things my sister and I did together when we were little.

Then he came out with the answer I was expecting from him regarding his theory of crime solving, 'Of course it is. How else would it work? There's your kill quest, delivery quest, gather quest. It's very straightforward Sam. Deconstruct it.'

I pretended to deconstruct the past week or so, 'So you're all playing me?'

'I'd prefer to think of it as playing with you.'

I pretended to be taken aback. I knew all this. But did they know I knew? Who were they? And why didn't Amos have a better grasp of the correct plot of the Maltese Falcon? I really should stop asking myself questions. It was giving me a headache.

Amos poured me a whiskey from a bottle in his desk drawer. Luckily his doctor's surgery was well equipped with the essentials. Amos seemed ridiculously thrilled with himself. He was like a scruffy little mixed mongrel that had brought the ball back for his master. I could see his little tail wagging and hear his little fucking barky voice. 'So you see Sam, we are all on the same side. Trust me. I'm an angel.' He roared with laughter at his wit and hilarity, 'Cheers.' He added.

I took a sip and feigned admiration, 'I see. But Amos, what is this list all about. You'll know. You're smart.' I showed him the list of red names from the folder;

Samyaza Watcher

Daniel Llewellyn

Amos Caddoc

Pedwar Penn

Barry Abloec

Mary Lileth-Llad

~~Cai Tywysog~~   Samael Watcher

He looked at it carefully, 'Ah. This is the committee list, Sam. Where did you get this? No matter. No matter.' He waved me away.

'This is next year's committee list. Interesting.'

'Interesting?'

'Yes, I thought Pedwar would be above me. Ah well. That's good.' He was thrilled.

'But what does it mean?' I asked,

'It's the committee list. The list of committee members.'

'Yes.'

'It's a group of people officially delegated to perform a function - investigating, considering, reporting, or acting on a matter.'

'I know what a fucking committee is.'

'And you're on it. In place of Cai.'

'But Cai's dead.'

'Yes.'

I muttered under my breath, 'Fuck me.' Then more loudly, 'I see Amos. But tell me a little more, Amos. Tell me something I don't know?'

'No. No. No.' He suddenly stood up ready to usher me out.

'You've said too much?' I asked hopefully?

'Oh no Sam. I've said exactly the right amount.'

'Amos. What exactly is your role in this village?'

'I have no idea. I've been told to wait. My time will come.' He grinned a shit-eating grin. We shook hands for some bizarre reason and I left. Rose and Seren were no longer there. Perhaps Rose was getting ready to come and work for me. Well that was one secret I had over Amos. He didn't know that did he? Oh, come on who was I kidding. Of course he knew.

I put on my hat and walked out.

THE DOCTOR'S TALE

I am the young one. I am the magick one. That was my gift, my skill, my way in.

I didn't get too involved in the struggle. I was young, but not radical or subversive. I just wanted a quiet life. To be honest I was mainly in it for the women. I loved women. Human women obviously. There were never any angel females which I thought was a bit ridiculous to me. I was taught that it was the way He wanted it. It would be too complicated. Well, I thought, if that's true why did He give us these urges. Then the women. They loved the magick. It's amazing how attractive you can look if you can do a little magick. I suppose I started it in a way. I was one of the first visitors. I was allowed. It was the shy, quiet one. The young one. I was showing off I guess and well she was enchanted by my magick. Literally and well..... What's an angel to do?

After the first it all kicked off and soon we were all involved and, well it did became a bit wild. At first we weren't sure if it was good or bad. Then He decided it was bad and it stopped. We heard the propaganda - all the children will be giants, deformed. We even believed it for a while. After a while, I guess, lust took over and well... the rest is recorded in the bible, fairly inaccurately if you ask me.

'And lawlessness increased on the earth and all flesh corrupted its way, alike men and cattle and beasts and birds and everything that walks on the earth all of them corrupted their ways and their orders, and they began to devour each other, and lawlessness increased on the earth and every imagination of the thoughts of all men was thus evil continually.'

I decided to stay with the other four. I liked it. I'm a little lazy and not as lustful as I was. Perhaps I'm growing up. Or looking to settle down. Whatever. I think I'll stay for a while. My ambitions lie in other directions now. One day, perhaps I could be the leader. Who knows? God knows?

27 They Kill Us for Their Sport

I walked along Waterloo Road until I reached the old ruins. Perhaps I
was caught up in the story now and I was looking for a clue, a blood-
stained handkerchief, a footprint or something. I wasn't. I did have a
quick look though then laughed at my stupidity. I had a very strange
feeling. I did keep reciting the Shakespeare lines in my head, 'As flies to
wanton boys are we to the gods. They kill us for their sport.' And
smiling.

'Amos told me Lily and Daniel were married.' I said out loud.

'I never knew Lily was married to Daniel' said Seren.

'Really? You must be the only one in Wales. I wonder why?'

'Because I'm a girl, obviously,' she said then went strangely
quiet for a minute.

I waited. 'It's so fucking typical of this place. Unless you can piss
standing up you don't get anything. I tell you, this village is the most
sexist place on the planet.' She paused, then added, 'or on any planet
or, or ...' she trailed off, then asked, 'Where are angels supposed to
live?'

I couldn't answer that, but had a stab, 'Apparently they move
between heaven and earth.'

She was not impressed and swore a few times. I had met my
sister a few minutes ago. She was already here, at the ruins. I wondered
if we had arranged to meet her. Or, if she had just happened to be here.
I was beyond caring, but thought I'd ask anyway.

'Anyway sis,' I neatly changed the subject, 'What are you doing
here?' I asked.

'Mind your own fucking business bruv' she said, not
unpleasantly.

We looked at each other. I spoke, 'Come on sis. This isn't going to work unless we trust each other, is it? We are partners after all.' I paused, 'and siblings.'

She considered.

'OK bro. I met Pedwar on the road outside Caddoc's house. He wanted to talk. Here. He told me that he saw Michael with Lily after the wedding.'

'Whoa. Whoa sis. Why did Pedwar want to tell you that?'

'I don't know'

'Where is he now?' I interrogated.

'Look, stop fucking interrogating me. Do you want to know or not?'

'Sorry. Go on.'

She looked a little lost. I prompted her, 'Michael?'

'Right. Well apparently when Lily stormed out Pedwar had gone after her. He saw Lily and Michael talking. Lily was really upset. Crying in his arms.'

'In Michael's arms? That's a bit of a cliché don't you think?'

'Of course.' She paused. 'It doesn't mean it's not true though?

'Do you believe it?' I asked.

'Why not?'

'Why would Michael be interested in Lily?' I asked a rhetorical question. My sister chose to answer it with one of her own, 'What do we know about Cai?'

'Well you know more than most I guess'.

She was now in question asking mode herself, 'But who is his father was for a start? He never talked about him. Not even when he was a kid. Why is that?' She continued and continued.

I tried to answer some part of it, 'I don't think he knew himself? His mum disappeared with our mum didn't she?'

'She did.'

Silence.

'Did Cai tell you anything at all, sis? Anything?'

'Nothing at all', she lied.

'Do you think Michael looks like Cai?' I asked, trying to lighten the subject.

Seren thought. 'I've never seen Michael that often. Pictures in the bible and all that. But now that you mention it....'

'Could he be Cai's dad?'

'Fuck.' Said Seren, 'That would be interesting.' She lit another Chesterfield and offered me one. I accepted. 'So if someone had killed your son you might be a bit pissed off.'

'And want to do something a bit biblical.' I replied.

'Like exact some revenge.'

We both smoked silently for a time. I changed the subject again subtly and tried to find more information about Seren's relationship with Cai. 'So were you going to marry Cai or what?'

'Who knows? Why do you care?' She answered crossly.

'Because I'm your brother and want you to be happy.'

'Really.'

'Really.'

She shrugged, 'That's nice Sam. But I'm sure as hell not going to marry him now, am I?'

She finished her cigarette, threw it on the floor and stamped on it. 'Come on, let's get back.' And she headed back home.

'I'll be right behind you sis.'

I thought a little and finished my cigarette. I threw it on the floor carefully then bent down to pick up my sister's cigarette butt.

I looked at it carefully. I took the butt I had picked up from the ruin the night Lily was killed. They matched. There was the same type of lipstick and tiny teeth imprints.

I run after my sister, 'Wait up sis.'

SUNDAY JULY 16th 1933

Bobby Jones' Remembers

Merion C. C. Pennsylvania Saturday September 27 1930

I was exhausted. I should be the happiest 28 year old in the world. I was slumped in the locker room at Merion Cricket Club, which was the golf club. I had just done it. I had completed the final part of the journey. I sat next to Harrison R Johnson. 'Jimmy' as he was known to everyone.

'Well done, Bobby'. He shook my hand, 'That looked easy.'

I had just smashed Eugene Homans 8 and 7 in the most one-sided final there has ever been in the US Amateur Championship. I had just completed an unheard of feat. I had won the US Open Championship, British Amateur championship and the Open to complete the 'Impregnable Quadrilateral' as it was known. Only later did it become known as 'The Grand Slam'. Added to that I had just won a bet of over $60,000. I was proud, but I didn't feel much like celebrating. It had been expected. People were asking what I would do when I won them all. Would I retire? Would I turn professional? I half joked that I couldn't afford to.

'It's all too much Jimmy.' I acknowledged. 'That's it. I'm through with golf. The strain of it all is killing me. It's ruining my health.'

Jimmy looked at me strangely. He had won the previous year but he would die to have a tenth of the fame and publicity I had.

'To tell you the truth Jimmy I'm sick of it.'

I wasn't just talking about the golf. I went out of the locker room to acknowledge the crowd. I lifted the cup and I knew that was it. It had been a long journey but somewhere inside me I knew it had to end. I was going home. Wherever that was.

115

I put on my victor's face and went out to meet the crowd. They were so happy for me. There was a guard of fifty marines that allowed me to get from the locker room to the edge of the green for the presentation. I shook hands with the President of the US Golf Association, Finley Douglas, and lifted the big, and heavy, Havemeyer Cup. The crowd were really loud and I forgot my tiredness. I was ecstatic. The only down side was that in all the pushy and shoving I'd somehow lost 'Jane'. I wasn't even bothered. We had reaching a natural end, I thought.

28 Honour Thy Father and Thy Mother

I opened the door of my Balaclava Road office at my usual time, nine o'clock precisely. Rose was there. She was making a great job of organising my non-existent filing system. She seemed to have created a folder for each case, or potential case. She had a book for my accounts - income and expenses, double-entry book keeping, no less, if that was the right term. It was stunning. Lily was efficient. It seemed Rose was super-efficient. She looked up briefly as I walked in.

'Coffee on your desk Mr Watcher.' She said tersely.

'Thanks' I mumbled, overwhelmed.

'And you've got a visitor.'

She was brusque, granted, but that was a small price to pay.

I sighed.

'Morning Aunty Mary,' I said as I entered the inner room.

I was wrong. It was my sister.

She poured over the notes and pictures from the folder. It seemed that she had somehow opened the safe somehow. Even though I assumed I had the only key. Obviously I didn't. I didn't even bother to ask. It would only make her lie and say that she didn't get a spare copy of the key from Uncle Daniel.

'Sam. I've decided I'm going to help you.' She said.

'I thought you were?'

'I'm going to help even more.' She smiled.

'I've found something out about our mother,' I said.

'Later Sam, me first.' She said then she handed me a list of dates and places my father had visited. The list I had written;

Transvaal 1895;

Shengting Province 1899;

Chihuahua 1910;

Sarejavo 1914;

Petrograde 1917;

Dublin 1922;

New York 1923;

Philadelphia 1924;

Columbus Ohio 1926;

Liverpool 1930;

Philadelphia 1930;

Wanpaoshan 1931;

Lausanne 1932;

Berlin 1933.

She looked like a lap dog waiting to be congratulated. I looked at the list without saying a word.

Seren looked puzzled. I shrugged.

'According to this,' she said excitedly. 'He's in Germany now.'

'So?' I asked.

'Well nothing. I just thought you'd be keen to know where our father was.'

I sighed. 'Is that it? Anything else?'

'Yes. Look at this.' She handed me a pile of invoices and receipts. 'Lily has signed all these receipts.' I looked hard at them. It was true. I recognised Lily's hand.

Seren continued, 'It seems Lily was more than your secretary. She seems to have been the family's secretary as well.'

'I thought Aunty Mary was?'

'It seems Lily was the secretary to the secretary.' I looked again. This was very interesting. I knew she would have been keeping an eye on me. Now, it seems, she was Aunty Mary's trusted right hand woman.

She had a lot more power than I had imagined. She was obviously working for Uncle Daniel as his spy with Aunty Mary as well.

Then it was my turn, 'There's this,' I took the list out of the envelope and showed Seren;

Samyaza L. Watcher

Daniel Llewellyn

Pedwar Penn

Barry Abloec

Amos Caddoc

Mary Lileth-Llad

~~Cai Tywysog~~ Samael Watcher

She took it from me and started reading it. She read it a number of times, looking for something.

I said, 'Amos told me this was the list for the future committee.'

'So where am I Sam? Where's my fucking name?' She paused. 'And anyway, what's this to do with our mother?'

'It's her writing' I said.

Seren was genuinely surprised. It was the first look of genuine surprise I'd seen since I returned. Seren looked at the list again. Then, silently, she took a photograph out of her bag. She showed it to me. It was a photo of our mother. I had never seen the photo before. It was a snap of me, my sister and mother on a beach somewhere. We looked happy. We looked warm. We looked like a proper family. My sister looked at me. I could see that her eyes were red, really red.

'This was taken the week before you left.'

I froze. 'What happened to her?'

'I don't know – she disappeared a few days later with Inanna, Cai's mother.'

She wiped away a tear. Then she looked at me to see if it was working. I wasn't going to cry if I could help it. I did feel sad though as it suddenly struck me that she had blamed me for our mother's disappearance. She must have held this grudge against me for a decade now. How could any of our previous life hold a candle to that feeling?

I was thinking about her past ten years. Her only friend was Cai. It's no wonder they became so close. And how angry she would be if anything happened to him.

I also remembered that the origin of 'holding a candle' was to do with an apprentice holding a candle for their master to allow them to work more accurately. Whose apprentice was I becoming? They had invested a great deal in my tutelage. By for what specific purpose? I tuned back in to Seren. She was still crying a little and talking a lot. It all had to be listened to through the filter of ten years of hatred now. I had lost her, I realised, and she was using me.

She told me that our parents had argued a lot over the years because of his work. Apparently he wasn't the easiest man to live with. He had a short temper, an obnoxious attitude and was inclined to be selfish. I had heard it all before from my mother.

'Tell me something I don't know about our mother.' I asked.

'She was kind, gentle.'

'That's not what I remember.'

'She was.'

'Really?'

She looked at me, reconsidered her lie and slowly replied, 'She was....She looked like Ingrid Bergman. Well maybe she wasn't that gentle though. She fought to keep you here.'

She handed me the photo. I looked carefully at it. She did look like Ingrid Bergman in the film Casablanca. 'Kiss me. Kiss me as if it were the last time.' She had the face of an angel, ironically. My mother not Ingrid Bergman. Well, both really. With that wide-brimmed hat, those lips and crying eyes.

Seren continued in similar vein, 'She loved you Sam. So much. She loved you more than anyone could in this world. She couldn't bear the thought of you turning into your father. She tried to stop it but our father's mind was set. She knew you were going away and that when you returned you would not be the boy you once were.'

I almost replied with, 'Let's face it sis. The problems of three little people don't amount to a hill of beans in this crazy world.' But I didn't.

I was impressed with the scriptwriter, or whoever it was writing Seren's lines.

'And....' I prompted.

'And then you went away after all the rows and arguments.'

'And mum?' I asked

'She went away too.'

'Where is she? I guess she's waiting for us somewhere.' I think this was too much. Too melodramatic.

Seren looked at me as if I were an idiot. She became genuinely tearful. Finally she went off message.

'She's dead obviously. He killed her.'

'But you don't just kill someone because of a few arguments.'

'When else would you kill someone?'

'You know what I mean.'

Then more quietly she said, 'you killed her.'

I accepted this. I had known it ever since I had returned and found she was missing. 'And you hate me?' I asked her.

Silence.

Then, 'Not just for that Sam.'

I waited.

'You hated Cai, as well. When you were sixteen you only became his friend because you knew I liked him.'

I didn't remember this. But, it seemed like something I would do to protect my sister.

'You did everything to stop him seeing me.'

I thought hard. It was possible I suppose. I decided to try as hard as I could not to ask any more questions. It only seemed to fire her up even more. Unfortunately I couldn't stop myself, 'But why are you telling me this now?'

'Because it's important – he's coming back for you soon.'

Silence.

I poured myself a bourbon straight up. I sighed. It looked like she was going to cry again. I didn't have time for this. I had a case to solve. My filial relationship problems could be sorted later.

I finished my drink and left. I couldn't bear to look at my sister. Guilt, I guess. I didn't hate her for anything – how could I? She hadn't done anything wrong – probably. But when I did look at her I couldn't remember her. I knew she hated me. I knew she had been used to manipulate me by someone. Judging by the speech, probably my old headmaster. I left her alone, either crying or pretending to cry.

I wandered along the road aimlessly. Then I decided to visit the golf club. I wanted to have a look at Calamity Jane again. I had a feeling it would be returning soon.

29 Sir Walter

I hiked up Mountain Road joyfully. The sun was shining. Really it was. I was quite chilled as I strode up the hill. I didn't think too much about my life, or Mynydd Eimon, my past life, my mother or my father. I didn't feel the need to smoke. I was enjoying the walk. I wasn't even too worried about my sister. I had little idea of what she thought of me or what I could have done differently to make her happy. I decided to let it go - for the moment. I did want to find the putter though.

As I reached the driveway to the golf club a large grey car practically knocked me over. I followed it cautiously along the drive. As I reached the clubhouse the large Daimler had stopped and someone was getting out. A largish dapper (that is the only word to describe him) man alighted regally from the dazzling three shades of grey Daimler saloon deluxe. He wore an immaculate white suit, dark grey brogues with a pale grey tie. He got out of the car, leaned against the bonnet and lit a large cigar. He surveyed his surroundings haughtily. He smoked slowly savouring every moment.

A few minutes later I saw Michael walking out from the clubhouse to greet him, extremely affably. I looked closely at the man from the Daimler. I knew him. I knew him extremely well. Michael shook his hand vigorously and I listen to them as I approached.

'Michael, how the devil are you?' said the Daimler man in a mild not unpleasant, yet American voice.

'Sir Walter. Delighted,' enthused Michael. 'Where have you been hiding?'

'Porthcawl. Dear boy. Lovely little place. Just lovely. But to tell you the truth Michael I'm a little tired.'

'Tell me, are you spending enough time with your family?'

'Not enough Michael, not enough. There's something I want to ask. A favour.'

'Of course Walter. Of course. Look, come inside and talk with me. Let's go to my room then go to the bar shall we? There's a drink with your name on.'

'Too kind, Michael. Too kind.'

'Walter,' said Michael, 'let me just take your golf bag and put it in the locker room'.

Walter opened the trunk of the car and Michael lifted the biggest golf bag I had ever seen onto the drive. He slung it over his shoulder and the pair of them strolled off together toward the bar without a look at me. I knew who it was. Walter Hagen. Sir Walter. Perhaps the most elegant, colourful golfer of the time, winner of eleven professional majors and golf's first true professional.

At the door Walter Hagen turned his head and spoke to me, 'Come on Bobby. We need to catch up.' And he disappeared into the bar.

I stopped. I lit a cigarette. I needed to catch my breath. I started having pangs again, 'Well that didn't last long' I said to myself.

30 Walter Hagen is in the house

As I entered the clubhouse bar Walter and Michael were sitting by the window looking out over the eighteenth green. Walter had a large brandy and a cigar. Michael looked like he had a soda water. They were laughing and reminiscing like they were long lost brothers. Human moths flew in from everywhere. They made a detour to the bar, then gathered around the flame that was Sir Walter. The more he talked the more the moths loved it. It was a sight to behold. I recognised most of them from the reception at the Lamb. Holding the best positions, that is, as close as possible to Sir Walter were Pedwar and Aunty Mary. Amos and Uncle Daniel was conspicuously absent. Of course the twins were in evidence.

I went to the bar and there was a large Four Roses waiting for me. I picked it up, sipped it and went to sit near the Walter and Michael table. Sir Walter was holding court, 'So I drove up to the club at Porthcawl...'

'Royal Porthcawl,' interjected Michael.

'Of course,' continued Walter, 'Royal Porthcawl. In the Daimler you know. Do you know I have no idea whose Daimler it is?' Michael half nodded to indicate that it was taken care of I get out. Walter smiled, 'Where was I? Ah yes, Royal Porthcawl. As I say I was a tiny bit late for registering you know, and toddle along to the secretary's office. Well, he's a bit of an officious bastard so he's staring at me in a proper 'I don't care who he is I'm going to have him' kind of way, you know?'

A chorus of agreement.

Walter took a drink and continued, 'He's obviously not impressed or anything and I know I'm in the doghouse. So I say to him 'Awfully sorry old boy but I got a little lost in the lanes, not a problem is it?' He says 'Name?' I tell him.'

'He didn't know who you were?' Dai Proper chips in,

'Well of course he does dear boy,' continues Walter, 'but you know he's just doing his job. Treating everyone the same - even me!'

Laughter all around.

Walter smiled, took another sip of his brandy and continued. 'I tell him and then he goes, 'Looks like you'll be teeing off at 7:30 in the morning tomorrow.' I look at him and say, 'Dear boy, we both know that's not going to happen.' He starts to argue about rules being rules and I say 'Dear chap. You can put me down for whatever time you like, but I won't be here before lunch, and if you don't want me to play then fine. Just you'll have to be the one explaining it to my public who pay to see me'. That shut him up for a moment'

'I bet it did,' said Dai Copy, 'What happened then?'

'Well,' Sir Walter continued, 'As I was leaving he said, 'Oh and another thing. As you are a professional, and not a member, you'll not be allowed to change in the locker rooms. You'll have to use the toilets like all the others.' I wasn't surprised. It's something I've grown used to. I didn't say a word. I bit my tongue and the followed day I arrived on time. Well oneish. I stopped the car outside his office. I climbed into the back seat and started undressing in my Daimler. I'd taken my shirt off and attracting quite a crowd when I started going for my belt. Well you should have seen the rush to get me into the dressing room.'

The crowd roared with laughter.

'And how did the golf go?' asked Amos.

'Terrible. I played like an absolute donkey. I couldn't hit a cow in the arse with a banjo.'

The crowd went wild.

He shouted at the barman, 'Could I have a bottle of Pfeiffer's dear boy?'

An hour of anecdotes later Sir Walter moved away from his

entourage and came and sat by me. Michael shadowed him. I was on the next table, close enough to listen, but not really relishing being associated with the group of fawning sycophants. Walter looked at me, 'So Bobby. How are you now? Gosh we had some battles didn't we?'

Michael corrected him, 'It's Sam Junior.'

Walter ignored him, 'You weren't well that last time I saw you.'

'I'm fine Walter', I said.

'Ah I see you've still got the watch.' I looked down at the watch on my wrist. It was a Movado watch with a brown leather strap, 'TIFFANY & CO' on the top. I didn't remember seeing it until I looked down a few seconds ago. 'Is it engraved?' I asked, beginning to undo the strap.

'God I hope not,' said Sir Walter, 'We're guys not dolls,' and he roared.

When he had recovered himself, he said, 'Bobby, I met that Amy Johnson girl down the road the other evening. You know her don't you? You used to be quite friendly with her once, didn't you? Charming girl. Utterly charming. She's just about to fly to America, you know? Single handed. Amazing'

'Right.'

'I've invited her to join us this afternoon to make up the fourball. Hope that's OK? Thing she's a decent golfer you know. Married to that chap, what's his name? Likes a bit of a drink.'

'Jim Mollison' said Michael.

'That's right', continued Walter, 'We've played with him. He's fun as I remember. Well he can't make it - meeting some lady he says. Not a word to Amy though'. He grinned and tap the side of his nose.

I had no idea who he was talking about, 'I don't think I've ever met them Walter.'

'Oh I'm sure we played with them a few times. Down South,

Sandwich area, I think. Ah well, never mind. She said she had a few things to do and would be with us in the hour.'

Michael was thrilled. He loved his golf and loved the talented and the famous. It's an angel thing I believe.

'Just time for a few more I think.' said Walter, 'another brandy here my good man,' he called to the barman.

I went along the corridor to see if 'Calamity Jane' had turned up. I needed a decent putter. There was no sign of it in the case. Amos was just coming out of the locker room. We greeted each other, fairly convivially. He informed me that he was excited. He was going to caddy for Sir Walter. I smiled, 'well done, you.'

'Thanks,' he said. He didn't understand sarcasm.

'Where's Walter's bag?' I asked innocently.

'I've put that somewhere safe, Sam. I saw it in the locker room and anyone could have taken it. You know what they're like around here?'

'I do. So, where is it now?'

'Safe in the secretary's office. Seren was in there and she said she'd look after it for me.'

'Excellent. Can't be too careful, can you?'

We shook hands. He likes that. I was about to go to the Secretary's office when I heard a car outside. I went out of the door and had a look.

31 Amy Johnson, Queen of the Air

A taxi pulled into the car park. Out stepped what looked like a tall, young girl. Her youth could not be attributable to her looks. She looked grown up. It was her shy awkward manner that gave the impression that she was young. She reminded me of a bird walking awkwardly on the ground, out of her graceful, natural habitat of the air. She looked around nervously, anxiously, unsure of her surroundings. As soon as she saw me her face changed. She rushed toward me, 'Bobby, Bobby. Hi. I'm so relieved to see someone. I had no idea where the taxi was taken me. Oh Bobby it's great to see you. Great to see you again.' She spoke in a breathless whisper. The driver opened the boot of the car. I paid him and took out her golf clubs.

When I turned around she was all over me again, 'Oh Bobby. How have you been? It's been so long. Five years. Five years. Can you believe it? Where have you been?'

'Where are you staying, um, Amy?' I have never seen this person in my life, I thought.

'Tenby.' She said, 'It's been a terrible few weeks. It's been terrible weather. Just waiting for the right weather is so, so boring. I saw Walter in Porthcawl and he invited me here. Just waiting for the right weather. I'm off to America you know?'

I did know. Walter had told me. I still had no real idea who this woman was. I did feel that I knew her though. I was a memory very like you get when you meet someone you used to go out with a long time ago. Someone you think you have forgotten. But you haven't. You remember the feeling, but not the person. It was a strange, complicated experience.

Amy went off towards the locker rooms. I had a memory of her always being in a hurry for everything. I had a chance to look at her as she talked to Amos at the clubhouse door. She wasn't cute, or attractive in a conventional way. But she had some vulnerability that attracted people to her. Well, me at any rate. As I looked at her I almost fell over, literally, as I felt a surge of memories flood into me. We had met in Blackpool. She really was a shy, young girl then. We had stayed in touch those weeks I had been over here as Bobby Jones in 1927 - Blackpool, Ascot, Scotland. We met once more in St. Andrews. Then I left. We became pen pals almost, with the occasional discrete phone call. It was more brother and sister to begin with. She must have reminded me of Seren at some level. She was fun. A welcome distraction. A link with the past. We both had our own lives but wanted each other. Then we had caught up at Sandwich, Kent at the Open a few years later and things had changed. Yes, I remember things had changed after that.

She was sitting on the wall outside of the club and smoking. The barman brought a drink out to her, and another for me. I sat beside her.

'I'm Sam, now, by the way.' I said.

She looked perplexed, 'Bobby?'

I felt sorry for her anxiety.

'Just joking. Anyway tell me about this trip you're taking.'

She told me about the weather and the problems for her at Pendine Sands. It was finally fine for her. She was due to leave tomorrow so needed to be back for a final dinner this evening. Her husband was with her but had a meeting somewhere. I sensed a definite note of sadness there. She livened up when I asked about the plane, the route and the danger.

Eventually Amy said, 'But Bobby what about you? How is Mary? How are the children? How's Clara? She must be nine by now?'

'Um. Yes. She must be,' was the best I could do.

'Do you miss me Bobby?' she asked quietly.

I stood up, 'Come on Amy let's get started. Walter would stay in the bar all day if we let. We need to shift him if you're going to get back in time for dinner.'

'Quite right.' She said. She stood up and went to the bar. I could hear her greeting Walter and Michael and the sound of happy laughter.

I went to the locker room and put my shoes on. I was close to tears now. I felt more and more little daggers stabbing, stabbing into me.

32 Golf Match

Amy had changed her shoes and was waiting alone on the first tee. I walked over to her.

'Walter said he'd be here in a minute', she said. Then continue, 'that was half an hour ago.'

I offered her a cigarette and we both smoked and chatted and waited. Michael walked out from the clubhouse with his clubs.

'Hello Michael.' Acknowledged Amy, 'Do you think Bobby and I could play against you and Walter?'

'That seems about right,' said Michael. 'How's your form?'

'So, so' said Amy, 'Not able to play too much recently, but you know.' She smiled, 'not too bad.' She was hopping from foot to foot excited to be up and running. She kept taking short, quick puffs on her cigarette and peering into the clubhouse looking for Walter.

We chatted and waited. By this time a decent crowd had gathered and it seemed they were going to walk along with us. Well, they were actually going to walk with Walter. They had already gathered near his golf bag. The biggest leather bag I had ever seen. Amos was caddying and seemed extremely excited at the prospect. He kept lifting the bag onto his shoulder, smiling, then putting it down. It was like all his Christmases had come at once. Angels really do love golf, you know.

Sir Walter wandered elegantly, unhurriedly out from the clubhouse in white trousers, monogramed silk shirt, two-tone shoes and gold cuff links.

'Hurry, please hurry,' breathed Amy.

Amy talked to me as Walter strolled to his bag, 'I need to get back to Tenby tonight.' she explained again, 'off to America in the morning, fingers crossed.'

We all shook hands amicably and wished each other to have a decent round, 'Ladies away.' Instructed Walter cheerfully.

Amy walked across the tee where Dai Proper handed her a driver.

Her drive went down the middle. She had a decent swing, elegant but lacking a little in power. I noted professionally.

I picked up a driver from Dai Copy, and drove. Straight as well.

Michael's caddy was Detective Inspector Eurion. He and Sergeant Rhydion had joined the crowd at some point. He handed Michael his club and Michael hit a great drive which landed past my ball.

Then laconically, Sir Walter wandered across and took a club from Amos' excited, but sweating hands. He hit a majestic drive straight and long down the fairway, 'I think I'll stop now,' he joked, 'I won't beat that one today.'

'Terrific shot.' said Michael.

'Thank you sir. I owe it all to you.' He smiled at Michael as if there were some secret between them. Which I suspect there was. The crowd laughed and moved off and we were away.

We walked along the fairway in our pairs. I felt happy talking to Amy as if we were old, old friends - which we were. There was a lovely, teasing, flirtatious tension between us that I had missed for so long.

We all got on the green in the regulation two shots and as I was furthest away I was the first to putt. I was looking at my shot when Walter approached with a putter.

'Think this is yours dear boy. I found it in my golf bag.'

He handed me 'Calamity Jane'. I looked at it carefully. There was a strange tingle as I held it. I quickly examined the old blade and spotted what looked like rust. Michael came over, 'Looks a little messy, Sam. Here let me.' And he wiped the blade clean with a cloth.

'Many thanks.' I acknowledged, 'I've been looking for this,' and I set about my long putt. I hit the putt from twenty feet. It would be great to say it went in, but it was close.

Walter won the hole with an amazing putt and we trooped off to the next hole. Walter was talking to an attractive lady from the crowd and Michael was in conversation with the policemen. The crowd were smiling and jostling to get the best view of Walter. Amy and I chatted about everything - golf, aeroplanes, Wales, the weather. Everything except Bobby Jones' family and her boyfriend. We delicately, mutually side-stepped the issue for the whole golf match.

The crowd loved Sir Walter. He talked to them constantly, answered their questions and smiled a lot. His round, amicable face beamed as he made some amazing shots. This would inevitably be followed by some self-depreciating remark.

He played without fuss. He offered Amos his club to 'have a go' when he hit a shot behind a tree, to the absolutely delight of the crowd. Amos blushed. Then Sir Walter looked at the ball, the tree and stroked his face. 'Any ideas?' he asked the crowd. Then he kept looking at angles and options, building the drama up more and more before selecting a niblick and hitting an enormous slice around the tree and onto the putting surface. The crowd went wild.

By the time we stood on the final tee we were level. The game had principally been between myself and Walter with Amy and Michael providing occasional support. We waited a while to catch our breath after climbing the hill from the seventeenth green. Walter was telling the crowd about his victory at the Open a few years back at Muirfield. Someone in the crowd said that he had been seen at midnight the night before the final round drinking. 'That's true dear boy.' He answered.

Michael said, 'and your opponent Leo Diegel. I heard he was in bed before nine.'

'He may have been in bed, dear boy, but he sure-to-God wasn't asleep.'

The crowd roared again. Walter then started his preparations for his final drive. He had one practice swing then hit an almighty drive down the centre of the fairway.

As Amy and I wandered down the hill towards the clubhouse she turned to me and said, 'Sam, we can get away, soon, can't we?'

I didn't know how or what to reply.

'I hate this circus of publicity, money, people, Jim. I love the flying, don't get me wrong, but please Sam. Rescue me.' She paused waiting for my reaction. I couldn't say anything so she continued, 'I just wish we could be alone and be happy somewhere. Once I've got all this aviation out of my system you will find a way for us to be together? Please?'

'But how could I do that?'

She smiled. 'Oh Sam. I'm sure you could do something as trivial as that if you wanted to.'

I smiled and gave her my new private investigator card, 'Let's talk about it, shall we? Call me.'

She beamed, took my card and rushed to play her ball from the edge of the fairway.

On the green I had a putt for the match. 'Calamity Jane' hadn't let me down all day and I knew I could putt this easily. I missed. The crowd groaned for a second, then cheered as Walter made his putt for the half and the match was drawn.

'Thanks Bobby,' smiled Walter, knowingly. 'The correct result I think.'

We shook hands warmly and wandered off the green.

'To the bar.' Instructed Walter.

'Have to dash', said Amy and she slipped off her golf shoes and put them in the boot of the waiting taxi. Dai Proper put her golf clubs in the back and she said goodbye to Walter and Michael.

'Be careful,' I said as we said goodbye.

'Always am' she smiled and kissed me once for luck, as she said.

'You be careful, Bobby,' she said getting into the taxi. With that she was gone.

I walked into the dressing room, took my shoes off and considered my options.

Bobby Jones' Remembers

Whitfield Estates Sunday February 28th 1926
Pasadena Yacht and Country Club Sunday March 7th 1926

It was cited as the heavyweight championship event of the golfing world. The battle of the Century to determine the best golfer in the world. I resisted it for a while. What did I have to gain from it? I know Walter wanted to play, and not just for the money - which was substantial. He wanted to beat me. He had the honour of his profession to fight for. In the eyes of the public Hagen was a brash, cocky, slick, showman, while I was modest, soft spoken, educated, and under stated. It was perfect for the media. They wanted a content of good versus evil, black against white, the light versus the dark. Me, the plucky, clean-living amateur against the black hatted villainous professional. As I say I had nothing to gain.

Then people started working on me and I did. I think it may have been my father who eventually persuaded me. Not my real father, but Robert Purdemus Jones, Atlanta lawyer. Although I have a feeling my real father had a hand in it. It would be a great chance to test yourself against the best in the world, was his argument. He became almost biblical in his advocation of the event. So I agreed. We had both been playing well and the public were mad for the event. Pages had been written. Eventually it was time to start. The first half would be in Florida, at my club. Then we would go to Walter's club in Pasadena. Well, to cut a long story short he walloped me. He beat me in my own back yard. I wrote later that 'Walter chopped my head off' and darn it that is exactly what he did. He played so well. He had the touch of the angels on him that first day. He outplayed me, outfought me and out-thought me. I'm sure I saw Michael those days hanging around the edges of the crowd. He was definitely with Walter at the end. Walter took the substantial cheque and bought me a handsome watch, which I truly appreciated.

There was a huge positive that came out of that day though. I had become a little too comfortable in my whole approach to golf. I was taking it all for granted somewhat. After this thrashing I worked harder. I got help from tommy Armour, a great golfer and friend. Who knows, maybe this was the spur I needed to improve to help me reach the dizzying heights I did.

33 Existential Argument with a Depressed, Paranoid Angel

I must have been in the locker room for a while. When I went into the bar Sir Walter had disappeared. Amos told me that his final words were, 'I'm going back to civilisation, dear boy. Or what passes for it here in Wales. I'm off to Cardiff.'

There were still a lot of people there. More even, than in the afternoon. This was not unusual. There was very little to do on a Sunday in Mynydd Eimon. Replacing Sir Walter was Uncle Daniel. I looked around for my sister. I wanted to talk to her about the few spots of red I had seen on my putter before Michael had wiped it off.

I took a deep breath, and a stiff drink, and sat myself next to my Uncle Daniel.

'Sam. Sam,' he started, 'How are you Sam? I hear you've been busy?'

'Really?' I said. 'Who's been talking out of school?'

Daniel laughed. He was more than a bit drunk. It looked like he'd been here the four hours or so we had played golf. 'You've been asking a lot of questions,' he continued.

I shrugged, 'It's my job.'

'Sam. I know you think you know a lot about Lily. And you know I paid her to.... to look after you. You're a detective aren't you?'

I nodded.

'Well detect her killer for me please. Will you?' he looked pathetic.

'I'll try Daniel, but I could do with a little bit of help. Please stop pissing me about moving me from person to person like a game of pass the parcel. If you want me to find Lily's killer you need to tell me what you know.'

'Oh. Tricky one,' he slurred, 'If I did that I'd have to kill you.' He laughed without any sense of happiness whatsoever.

'I'll have to kill you.' he repeated, waiting for a reaction from me.

I did my best impression of someone bored talking to a drunk person.

'Sorry Sam. Just a joke.' He mentally pulled himself together. 'OK what do I know?' Then without waiting for an answer he answered his own question, 'I know that you know about Lily's involvement in... the family business. She looked after the invoices with Mary. So what? That's not enough to get her killed though. Is it?'

'I think Lily's murder was a direct result of Cai's.' I said, 'what else do you know Daniel?'

'I know Michael killed Lily, if that's any help.'

This was a little direct for Daniel.

'Really?' I said. I don't think so. Why would he do that?'

'He must think somehow that we killed Cai.'

'We?'

'Lily and me. Me and Lily. Lily and I. All six of us.' Again he laughed.

I considered Michael thinking Lily and Daniel killed Cai. I'm pretty sure he could kill someone, but Lily? He'd be more inclined to kill Daniel, I thought. Then I asked, 'Now why would he think that?'

'Well because I sort of did.' He said. He paused for dramatic effect, 'Well. I sort of didn't as well. We all know Mary killed him, right. But... but.' He stopped in the way only drunken people can stop when they need to work out how to finish the sentence they had started, 'but maybe she was influenced by someone, or sometwo.' He thought this was hilarious.

'Now why would Michael care about that?'

'Ah. Ah' he said, followed by a dramatic sweeping gesture, 'That is the question. Why indeed? Why does he turn up here now? A place he has rarely visited in eons. Why did he send Stan and Ollie to come and look menacing trying to scare the muggles and half-muggles?'

He laughed again. This is now borderline hysterically funny to him. People are pretending not to listen. Getting nothing from me he decided to answer his own question, 'He's making a statement.'

'And the statement is....?' I prompted.

'You know Sam. You guessed early on. Revenge. 'Vengeance is mine, sayeth the Lord."

He stopped, 'And I'm next.' He went a little quieter now. He descended into that drunkard's little self-centred universe of me, me, me.

'You don't know that.'

'Don't I? I wonder what happens to us when we die?' he said, mainly to himself. 'We can't go and join the angels can we?' He laughed to himself, more quietly, thoughtfully.

'But aren't angels immortal?'

'You'd think so wouldn't you? Alas no. Only fame lives forever.' He laughed.

He took a long drink then stood up, and recited something from somewhere 'You are gods, and all of you are children of the Most High. But you shall die like men, and fall like one of the princes.'

'You're mortal.' I said, 'So have any of you died?'

'Not yet. Oh Sam I wish your father were here. He could save me.'

We sat and drank in silence for a little while. I knew all of this to be true. I was quite pleased to have the confirmation though. I was surprised Michael had taken it so seriously though, even if he was Cai's father.

'So what's going to happen? I still don't understand why Michael

141

would want to kill you?' I asked.

He poured himself another drink.

'Because we killed his son, didn't we.'

This I knew. I didn't want to know the answer to the next question, even though I did, but had to ask it anyway, 'Why did you kill Cai?'

Daniel sighed. 'To make room for you, of course. The great Samael. The Chosen fucking one. 'And he will call all the Host of the Heavens and all the Holy Ones above, and the Host of the Lord, the Cherubim, and the Seraphim, and the Ophannim, and all the Angels of Power, and all the Angels of the Principalities, and the Chosen One, and the other host that is upon the dry ground, and over the water, on that Day. And it will come to pass in those days, that neither by gold, nor by silver, will men save themselves; they will be unable to save themselves, or to flee." He sat down, 'it's all part of his plan.'

'No. God. Who do you think? Of course your father's.'

He took another big drink, 'We've lost' he said.

I was bored of this self-pity now. I wanted to do something better than have an existentialist argument with a depressed, paranoid angel.

I left. On the way out I said goodbye to Daniel and said, 'You know what Daniel I think I will take that job as golf professional you offered me. I'm sure I could do more than one thing at a time'.

I needed a priest.

THE SOLICITOR'S TALE

It was my job to get us away and keep us safe. I was the safe pair of hands. I was the sidekick. The Boswell. The Tom Hagen. 'The woman behind the throne', they joked behind my back. I got us all to Mount Eimon, Wales and built this community. I decided who stayed and who went. I had to make the wives disappear. I had to do everything he said. And I did. Everything he said.

I really, really was the real power behind the throne. Honestly. I made the magick happen. Made up the rules. When we could use it, when we couldn't. I was the police. Keeper of the keys. I was the chief Administration Officer supreme. I was happy enough playing second fiddle - for a while. But I had my needs too. Don't you think I didn't want to explore, to spread the word? Of course I did, but I was the server. But I hoped I would have a son who would take the lead. But it didn't happen and I was the 'uncle'. He wanted his son to lead. I obeyed, of course. I trained him - nurtured him - sent him away to learn - brought him back and now he hates me for it. In the end I couldn't even save my own wife.

34 Do Angels Leave Footprints?

'Barry. Tell me about the bible.' I had left the golf club and was visiting Father Barry. I decided that my style for dealing with him would be... direct.

'Father Barry.' He corrected.

'Father Barry. Tell me about the bible.'

'Which bit?'

'The Book of Enoch.'

'It is said that he was a cobbler you know.' Father Barry sounded knowledgeable.

'But he wasn't was he?' I replied. I wasn't in a particularly good mood.

Father Barry went quiet, 'He wasn't.'

He recited, "Then said the Most High, the Holy and Great One spake, and sent Uriel to the son of Lamech, and said to him: 'Go to Noah and tell him in my name 'Hide thyself!' and reveal to him the end that is approaching: that the whole earth will be destroyed, and a deluge is about to come upon the whole earth, and will destroy all that is on it.'

I waited for him to finish, 'No before that.'

Father Barry was in his church with me. We were standing near the altar. He loved the sound of his own voice, especially in the cavernous space of this old church.

Father Barry continued, 'Ah but this is relevant. This is the point we're going toward. It's the end of the beginning.'

I had had enough of this enigmatic nonsense. I decided to express myself assertively. I reached out and coolly grabbed Barry by the throat and whispered, 'Barry. Just fucking tell me.'

He tried to get away and blustered in a thin, evil character cartoon way. I let him go and he shook himself like a dog. 'Just like your father', he announced as his smoothed his collar.

He calmed himself and continued, 'its part of the story. The ark, salvation, gopher wood, golf, St. Andrew, St Andrews. You've got nearly all the pieces now Sam. You're good at puzzles aren't you?'

'I thought I was.'

'It's all there; 'And it came to pass when the children of men had multiplied that in those days were born unto them beautiful and comely daughters. And the angels, the children of the heaven, saw and lusted after them, and said to one another...."

I finished the reading for Barry, "Come, let us choose us wives from among the children of men and beget us children.'

There was a pause. Then Barry spoke, 'Yes. You are one of the begotten.' He announced this triumphantly and redundantly.

I was bored. I looked up at Barry. He was no help. I started to walk away. Father Barry chased after me, almost desperately. I realised he was terrified of me for some reason.

'Sam – you know the truth already. You just don't want to accept it. Accept it.'

I stopped and turned. I did know the truth but it was so ridiculous to me - angels, Bobby Jones, murder, archangels. I needed one thing to make it all make sense.

'Tell me about angels?'

'What?'

'What do they look like Barry? Do they have wings?'

He laughed, 'No Sam. We don't have wings. We look as normal as you and I,' he paused, 'or your father or Amos or Daniel or Cai. ' He paused to consider his next line. 'We have to travel by train. We're not Spidermen or demons. We can't read minds or kill people with a single thought or leap tall buildings.' He considered some of the plus points, 'we can mess with time - bring bits of the future forward. Anticipate. We can be quite manipulative.'

'Really? You surprise me.' I was being sarcastic.

'Do angels leave footprints?' I asked casually.

'Of course. We're have mass, don't we?'

I think this was a joke. I looked at Father Barry carefully.

'No. It's not a joke. We have weight, mass, substance. If you prick us do we not bleed? Etcetera, etcetera.'

I decided to keep asking. I was on a roll now, 'So what happened with my father and Cai's father?'

'Ah Michael'.

He recited, 'Samael took hold of the wings of Michael whom he wished to bring down with him in his fall; but Michael was saved by God.' He paused.

'However that's not strictly true.' He explained.

'How do you know?'

'I was there. Or at least this was how it appeared to me in a vision when I wrote it. But I made up the last bit.'

'About God saving him?'

'Yes.'

'So what really happened then?'

'They had a fight and he fell off a cliff.'

'Really. Sam and Michael had a fight?'

'Of course. Sort of. Sam landed on Michael who was hurt. It was an accident.'

'And you know Enoch wasn't a cobbler because...'

'Because it was me. I was Enoch. I'm the only immortal one.'

'I know.' I said, 'and you think you are special, better than us don't you?'

'I am'. He said.

146

I looked at him. He was totally serious, about everything.
I left before my head exploded.

THE PRIEST'S TALE

I saw it all. The fight, the flight - the immortal being mortal because He decided.

This vengeful, revengeful arrogance piece of diety.

Michael and Sam, Cai and Samael, Ishtar and Inanna I knew them all.

I was the scribe, the watcher, the grigori, gwyliwr, iyrin, Enoch.

I was in Nebuchadnezzar's dreams. He decided that I would be immortal. The only immortal one. I was His favourite. So I can keep an eye on them. The fallen ones, the chosen ones.

He hasn't abandoned them. He loves them. He wants them to succeed. It's a test.

He told me. I am special. I am the one and only.

35 My Sister Coughs

I left the golf club and walked down the hill. I didn't know if Daniel would be OK or not. I doubted it. There was nothing I could do anyway, even if I wanted to. It's not that I was terrifically bothered either way.

I was more concerned with understanding Lily's death. I couldn't imagine Michael killing a 'civilian'. Whether this was because I'd read too many Mafia books, or what, I wasn't sure. Although, technically Lily had been married to Daniel, she was still a civilian. She had been made to do the things she did for her husband. It wasn't that I thought Michael was incapable of killing. I knew he was, but it didn't feel quite right to tell you the truth.

I walked down Mountain Road, along Waterloo Road and Lucknow Lane to my sister's house. Seren was alone. She had been crying.

She offered me a drink. I took up the offer.

I offered her a cigarette. She took up the offer.

'How was your game?' she asked

'Interesting. Why didn't you come to the club?'

'I don't like golf.'

'But it's not too often we get a few celebs in Mynydd Eimon.'

'A drunken old fart and a simpering bimbo?'

'So you did see them.'

She laughed.

'No. You were there weren't you, sis. Amos saw you.'

She said nothing. I changed tack. 'How close were you to Cai, sis?'

'Close enough. Why? What do you care?'

'I've been paid to solve the murder.'

'Paid?'

'By Aunty Mary.'

She laughed again.

'Why did you do it sis?' I asked.

'Do what?'

'Kill Lily.'

'Because I loved him and that evil bitch murdered him.' She stated calmly.

'But Aunty Mary did.'

'But we both know she was pushed.'

'Yes, but you got the wrong pusher.' I said.

Seren stopped smoking.

'Who's the right pusher Sam? Who pushed Lily's button? Aunty Mary? Daniel? Dad? You? Where do you stop?'

'At Lily apparently.' I stated.

'Daniel made her. You know that.'

'I do now,' she said, 'I didn't on Saturday. I didn't even know they were married.'

She stubbed out her cigarette and took out a Chesterfield. I took one as well.

We lit it and she saw me looking, very pointedly, at the cigarette.

'Most people smoke Chesterfield's in Mynydd Eimon. That's not proof.' She paused, 'Look I saw you do all that detective work at the ruins, but that's not proof.'

'But it was you wasn't it sis.'

'Do you want me to ask you, 'How did you find out?'?'

'Yes please.'

'Fuck you.'

I ignored her, 'I suggest it was Seren who did it in the Ruins with the golf club. You could at least have wiped the blood from my putter.'

She sighed, 'It's a fair cop gov. So, what will you do?'

'Nothing of course. This is Mynydd Eimon after all.'

'She was a right bitch though.'

'But it wasn't her fault sis, was it? You know that. She was innocent.'

Seren was quiet.

'She wasn't so innocent.' Then added, 'She was a bitch though wasn't she?'

I felt this had been crossed off my list, and found myself wondering, 'and so what?' I saw my Seren finished her cigarette. She had no remorse. No guilt. No feeling at all for killing someone.

'I need to see Daniel.' I said.

'Should I come?'

'No, sis. I need to do this. I'll see you later.'

36 Your Mother is Safe Sam

I went back to the golf club. It was still early evening and as I said there's not a lot else to do in Mynydd Eimon on a Saturday night. I was curious about Daniel. Not compassionate, just curious. He had hurt me a lot and I would never forgive him. I knew that. I had a drink and wandered into the Secretary's office. Michael was there sipping a club soda and staring out of the window.

I sat down opposite him. 'What's going to happen to Daniel?' I asked.

'It's OK. I'll take care of it. I always liked him.' Michael said.

Michael was pensive for a moment. Then he wasn't. The subject of Daniel was now closed.

'I'm leaving in a minute' he said, 'How did it ever come to this?' he continued.

I listened. It seemed the best thing to do.

'I've lost a son and he's gained a son. I won, for God's sake. We never used to be like this. We used to be so close, shared the same values.'

'Where is he, Michael? Where's my father?'

'I honestly don't know. Swear to God.'

I believed him, 'and my mother?'

'Your mother? I loved her, once.'

I must have looked surprised.

'No. No. Nothing like that. I loved her sister Inanna, romantically. But we had to hide it. Sam helped me hide it from Him, for a while.'

'How come you didn't get, er.' I struggled for an appropriate word, 'banished?'

I felt like he wanted to tell me. Then he said, 'Well that's a long story from another time.'

I must have looked disappointed. He threw me a bone, 'Your mother is safe Sam. So is Cai's mother. Both far away from your father.'

I stood up.

37 I Knew it was you, Daniel. You Broke My Heart

I went into the bar with Michael.

We sort of said goodbye. 'Excuse me', he said and walked off to sit by Daniel, who was sat at a table on his own, drinking and looking morose.

I went to the bar for a drink. It was quieter here now. Most of the people had left and there was a feeling that the circus had left town, or at least were packing their tents away. I saw Michael sit next to Daniel. They talked. I move a little closer and sat next to Pedwar who is chatting to Aunty Mary. They looked tense.

I couldn't hear any of the conversation between Michael and Daniel. Michael had such a quiet voice. Then Michael stood up and said 'There's a car waiting for you outside to take you to the airport.' I got goose bumps. For one instance I was tempted to take Michael aside, talk to him, plead with him. But I don't.

He left with Detective Inspector Eurion and Sergeant Rhydion. I tracked them at a discrete distance. Uncle Daniel got into the car. I watched from the doorway, smoking a Lucky Strike.

As the car pulled off I saw Seren. She noticed the car as it briefly drove past her. She paid it little attention. She was excited and has something to tell me. No sense of guilt or remorse, yet then.

'Oh Sam.' She said She had a piece of paper, 'I thought you'd like to see this'. She handed me a list of names and then turn around and walked back down the drive. It was the amended list of future committee members;

Samyaza Watcher

~~Daniel Llewellyn~~ Samael Watcher

Amos Caddoc

Pedwar Penn

Barry Abloec

Mary Lileth-Llad

~~Cai Tywysog~~   Seren Watcher

38 Father and Son Reunion

To the side of the eighteenth green there is an old elm tree. Next to the
tree is a garden type of area, a number of small bushes, rough unkempt
ground and so on. When you play golf you don't want to be there. But
tonight I did. It's quiet, peaceful, there's a bench there. I walked from
the clubhouse toward the bench. I sat on the bench and lit a cigarette.
That was when I saw my father in the garden. He was standing under
an elm tree smoking – half turned away from me – unaware. He did look
like Nosferatu. He really did, which was strange in that he wasn't that
skinny, but he had long, skinny fingers holding a long, skinny cigarette.
It must have been that which accentuated it. He seemed to have evil
seeping from every pore. He turned to me.....

No he didn't.......he looked incredibly normal. He had a dark suit
and a small goatee with accentuated the smallness of his mouth. He was
smoking under the elm tree though - a small cheroot, I think... He
turned and saw me and moved, almost glided, he did – he almost glided,
toward me. I had no idea how old he was. How did age work with
angels? He looked about fortyish. His last few steps toward me were
slower. He seemed almost wary of me.

His face said sorry before his mouth did. I had no idea what to
do. So I asked the question. I did.

'What about my mother?' I asked.

'Human' was the reply.

'Me?'

'Who knows? Never happened before. Maybe you'll take after me
or maybe your mother......' He stopped.

'Tell me about my mother?'

'No. I can't. She's gone.'

I waited.

'I loved her. I give up Heaven for her. Well it wasn't that much of a sacrifice. I was fed up anyway. I needed space. Needed to move. Branch out of my own. My work Sam. It's important. Especially now.'

'She's somewhere safe.' I said.

Sam smiled, 'Don't believe everything Michael says though will you?' He paused. Then continued, 'I need someone to manage things here while I'm away. It's going to be a busy time, 1933.'

He smiled.

I didn't.

'Your sister is going to be a big help to you Sam. She has amazing potential. She's much tougher than you.'

'So why not let her be in charge? I want no part of this.'

'Oh Sam. You are perfect. You've had the training, the experience. I've invested a lot in you.'

'So when is someone going to tell me about the years I've lost?'

'Oh Sam. We have an eternity for that. We need to concentrate on your current situation.'

I asked him about Father Barry, 'What about Barry?' I asked.

'I'll take care of Barry.'

I thought hard as he lit another small cheroot without offering one to me.

'What about Cai and Lily and Daniel?' I asked.

'I'd say it's working out rather nicely at the moment.'

'But your best friend is dead and it looks like it's all going to kick off in heaven again.'

'Yes'

'What will happen? Whose side will the angels be on? All against you I guess?'

'Us?'

'No. No. No.'

'What do you think I've been doing for centuries, Sam? I've been preparing for this. I've been lining up the dominoes. It's been difficult getting all the dominos in a row. Then I just needed to tip the first one.'

'What was the first one?'

'You. You came back.'

I didn't hug him, or hit him. I didn't say, 'Oh father forgive me for I have forsaken you,' or 'fuck you'. I just walked past him and went down Mountain Road, along Waterloo Road and Lucknow Lane to the old ruins to look for Seren.

Proof

Made in the USA
Charleston, SC
07 August 2015